THE HEALERS SOCIETY

A Short Novel

Laura Clementz

Disclaimer

This is a work of fiction. All the names, characters, businesses, places, events, and incidents in this book are either the product of the author's imagination or used in a fictitious manner. Any resemblance to actual persons, living or dead, or actual events is purely coincidental.

Laura Clementz
Bright Communications LLC
Cleveland, Ohio

The Healer's Society
ISBN 978-1-7340497-9-4

A Note from Joanna

MY NAME IS JOANNA. As the oldest healer in our group and the second healer in my family, I was the obvious candidate to document our story; the story of how we came to find each other and how the Healer's Society came to be. I'm making the most out of the quietness during the late hour, typing with quick fingers and using eyes that have seen so many things. They are the eyes of a healer. We see beyond the skin, into the body, and the illness where it lies within. Sometimes the illness shows up as black discoloration that is distinct, laden with fuzziness or even with tiny arms that creep around like a ten-legged spider. Then, if we are lucky, we have the chance to heal the body. My memories go back to a time before complex wireless networks, cell phones in every pocket, and the explosion of social media to begin our story.

It Was Strange

JOANNA MANEUVERED CLOSER TO the booth and steadied herself on the last chair at the counter. Crystal, the other server working at the Wayside Retreat Diner that night, noticed her and met Joanna's eyes. Joanna gave Crystal a nod so subtle it was barely noticeable. When Crystal returned a small smile and went back to casually chatting with the middle-aged couple she was waiting on, Joanna knew she got the message. The two of them had worked together so long that they developed an intimate intuition for getting more than just the food on the table.

Joanna shifted a bit more so she could see as much of the man as possible and rested part of her body on the chair. She returned her stare to him, but this time let the rest of the world disappear. There was only her and the middle-aged man sitting at the booth.

Soon she could see inside his body. It always came in white and grey tones that outlined bones and major organs in a foggy haze. And somewhere in the haze would be a black deeper than the feathers of a raven sitting in the afternoon sun. She waited and could see a clear but small black area in the man's midsection, probably involving his stomach.

Joanna stared at the spot, stared at it hard. Never losing her concentration, she focused her energy, and like the other times before, something happened deep inside her brain. An odd sensation that her mind could squeeze the black illness until it disappeared. Her mind squeezed harder and harder and even harder. Meanwhile, heat rose-up her body and her chest filled with love. In reaction to an intense release, her head spontaneously snapped back, and her ears begged for mercy from a high-pitched ring. Finally, everything went dark for a splinter of a second and, besides being a little lightheaded, it was over.

Crystal had always been great at chatting with customers. She kept on engaging the couple while keeping a corner of her eye on Joanna. After the quick motion of Joanna's head, she turned her body, so she was blocking everyone else's view of the man as much as possible. The man bounced a little upward out of his seat as the unseen force thrust him. He let out a strange yelp and leaned forward while clutching his hands on the edge of the table.

"Everything alright?" Crystal asked him in an up-beat tone.

The man took a few deep breaths and sat straight. He looked at Crystal with confusion roaming in his eyes. "Yes, I think so. It was strange, like someone punched me in the stomach but it didn't hurt," he responded before he brought his napkin to his mouth and cleared his throat.

"Let me refill your water," Crystal said. As she left, she warmly smiled at his wife who was eyeing her husband from the other side of the table with concern. Crystal went to the server station for the water pitcher. Joanna was already waiting there with a generous slice of pie, napkins and two forks, which she handed to Crystal.

Not a bit different from how she was every day, Crystal returned to the table, filled the couple's water glasses with steady precision, and placed the slice of pie in between them. "Now, here you go. A piece of fresh apple pie on the house." She arranged a napkin and fork in front of each of them. "Enjoy and let me know if you need anything else."

Joanna went back to rotating through the rest of her tables. After getting through the third table, she glanced over to see the middle-aged couple happily sharing the pie. She smiled to herself and moved on to the booth where Lucinda was sitting, but Lucinda was nowhere in sight. She left a tuft of lettuce on the fork and a stack of money on top of the check. Joanna counted the money, and it was more than enough to pay for the bill. She felt a sickly churn in her stomach and looked around the diner.

Joanna walked outside, scanning the parking lot with her eyes. She didn't even know what Lucinda's car looked like and didn't see her anywhere. There was something about it that made her feel uneasy, but she returned to the insides of the diner. That's when she almost bumped into the middle-aged couple.

"I told you, honey, I feel great." The man said to his wife before noticing Joanna in their path. They maneuvered around her, making a quick stop to look at a few items in the small gift shop.

"Have a good evening," Joanna said to the couple right before they disappeared out the door. Done with her shift, Crystal followed shortly after them, giving Joanna a smile and a wave goodnight.

Travis was one of Joanna's last tables for the night. In high school, he was a well-known linebacker on the football team, but now he worked construction jobs in town. His shoulders were so broad that they spanned over half the booth and his body so large his stomach skimmed the table when he sat. Even more so, he gave off an aggressive energy that could fill the entire room. While hunching over his food, his black hair was the most predominate feature on his head.

"How is everything, Travis?" asked Joanna.

Travis took a hearty bite of his double cheeseburger and grunted with a full mouth, "It's fine." Then he continued with the fries by the handful.

"Say, did you happen to see where Lucinda went?"

"I haven't gotta clue." He scraped the last of the fries from the basket, then held it out to Joanna without looking up from the rest of his food. "Hey honey, would you fill my basket?"

She took the basket while shooting him a displeasing look but said with her regular voice, "Sure, I'll be right back with more fries." As she walked away, his radiating energy crept up her back until she involuntarily shivered.

She Wasn't Leaving

IT WAS DARK OUTSIDE when Joanna got home from work and closed the front door with a thump. She placed her bag on the floor and could hear Sanders shuffling around the kitchen. Sanders moved in about a year after they started dating and had lived with her for about three years. As she walked into the living room of the old two-story house, he poked his head around the entranceway.

"Hey baby, how was work today?" Sanders asked.

Joanna plopped down on the couch and took off her shoes. She looked at him and took in his handsome baby face topped with perfectly styled brown hair. His button dress shirt accented his strong shoulders. "It was good, pretty typical. I just feel a little beat."

"How about I get you a glass of wine? I just opened a bottle."

"Sure, that would be great." Joanna put her feet up on the small pincushion footstool that had been part of the house since she was a little girl.

Sanders returned with a glass of wine in each hand. He handed one to Joanna and sat down on the couch close to her. He took a few slow sips from his glass. "Feeling better yet?"

"I'm getting there…" Joanna sipped her wine, then gave him a playful look while tilting her head to the side. "Is there something going on?"

"I have some news."

"It's good news, I hope."

"Yes, excellent news."

Joanna set her wineglass on the coffee table in front of the couch and turned to give Sanders her full attention. "Let's hear it."

"I got a job with Canwell Accounting at their satellite office, here in Lightmeadow, as a Financial Manager."

"You're kidding!"

Sanders shook his head back and forth, his smile growing. "No, not kidding at all. They want me to start right away."

"Oh, honey." Joanna leaned over and gave him a hug. "I'm so happy for you." She settled back in the couch cushions and tugged at his shirt sleeve. "See, going to school all those years, completing the internship, and all the hard work is paying off."

"Yes." He looked her deep in the eyes. "Thank you. I couldn't have done it if it wasn't for you."

"You're welcome. I did it for us." Joanna was smiling so wide her eyes got watery.

"Speaking of us. Once I get started, you could leave your job at the diner. You wouldn't have to do it anymore."

"Well, I wouldn't want to leave completely." Joanna picked up her glass and leaned back into the couch. "But it would be nice to cut back on my hours to do more gardening and stuff around the house."

Sanders scratched the side of his head. "That wasn't what I was getting at. I know we've talked about this before, but if all goes well, I could get promoted to a position in Helinas."

"Helinas? That would be such a long commute for you."

"Yes, it is a long commute." He nodded a few times and returned her gaze. "So, I was wondering if you would reconsider moving to the city."

"Oh." Joanna paused and took a sip of her wine. "My life is here. My friends, my job, the house, it's all here. And I'm not a city girl. You know that."

"Well, maybe it's time to expand. Have some new experiences. I know you love the house, but don't you think it's time to move on? I mean, your grandmother and mother both died here. It's a little creepy."

Joanna turned away from Sander's widening eyes. His words sent a pain into her heart. He was right. She would be the third generation of women who have taken care of the house and lived within its walls for their entire life. But that was exactly the point. She wasn't leaving.

Joanna met his full gaze before saying, "You know how much the house means to me. It's a part of me. Part of who I am."

He looked down at the floor. "I know. I'm sorry, I shouldn't have brought it up again. Especially since it's not a concern right now." He took a sip of wine and flashed his most charming smile. "How about I draw you a nice hot bath so you can relax?"

"That sounds heavenly. I'll add my scented bath salts." Joanna leaned closer to him, and he responded likewise. Her hand rubbed his knee and moved up his thigh. "I love you, honey, and I'm so happy for you. This is an incredible opportunity." She gave him a soft, lingering kiss and felt his lips curve around hers.

JOANNA LOWERED HER BODY into the bathtub with the smells of sandalwood and bergamot drifting upwards along with the steam from the water. She closed her eyes and relished the warmth penetrating her skin until thoughts started coming into her mind.

She was happy for Sanders and the job he landed. They had talked about marriage a couple of times, and she had hoped that's where the conversation would go after he shared the news, but it didn't. Worse yet, he brought up moving to the city again. She wondered if he would ever be happy staying in Lightmeadow.

Her memory brought up a time when they were dating. Joanna had taken him to the meadow. She guided him through the hiking trail, pointing out different plants, flowers, bugs, and butterflies. Sanders had looked so enticing in the sunlight, that is, until he swatted his hand around his head to shoo something away.

"So, this is your thing? You don't mind the pollen or dust?" He leaned back as a bee buzzed by his head. "Or the bees?"

"No, I love it." She laughed and grabbed his hand. "The bees won't hurt you. They're here for the flowers."

At the end of the hike, they moseyed their way back to the car and leaned against the hood. "How about I make you a deal?" Sanders inquired.

"What's that?" Joanna asked.

"How about you can come here anytime you want; I'll never complain." Sanders slid closer and put his arm around her, pulling her against him. "But I won't come with you. It'll be your special outing." After a pause, he brought a flower up with his other hand and tickled it in her face.

Joanna laughed and leaned back as far as his arm would hold her. "Okay, okay. It's a deal." She sat up and he leaned in for an intoxicating kiss.

Her mind returned to being in the bathtub. She wondered if she should have known back then that things between them could eventually come to an impasse. It was too much to think about, so she let herself succumb to the hot water until it got cold.

I Just Had a Moment

AFTER A DAY AWAY from work, Joanna returned to the Wayside Retreat Diner for another shift. It's the busiest place in the town of Lightmeadow and sits off Interstate Fifty-Eight at the last exit before the highway splits to the north and south. Along with the local customers, many travelers visit the diner for a home cooked meal. Some are truck drivers making a living, some are vacationers headed to the Balmar Cascades National Park to the north, some are people headed to the large city of Helinas to the south, while others have their sites on destinations further away.

When he was a teenager, Gus started at the diner as a prep cook for his uncle. Eventually under the blessing of his uncle, he took the place over. To mark the change, he gave the diner a complete remodel. Gus kept the traditional diner seating including swivel chairs with low backs at the counter and comfortable booths that line the front wall next to the windows, all upholstered light blue with silver framework. He covered the walls with updated art déco wallpaper and pictures accented with deep grey tones. It was a lively, yet comforting place, complete with the intermingled smell of fluffy pancakes, sizzling patty melts, and warm apple pie.

Joanna was in the break room with Crystal getting ready for their shift. In contrast to Joanna's soft wavy reddish-brown hair that she kept short; Crystal puffed the wild curls of her long blond hair with a spritz of mega-hold hairspray before loosely pulling them back just above her hairline. With that complete, she pulled her makeup bag out and refreshed her bright pink lipstick. She performed all of this while happily chattering on about her date the previous night and periodically giggling so her long silver earrings jiggled back and forth.

Joanna didn't keep a complete focus on Crystal's words because, although lively, Crystal has told similar stories many times only with different characters. Joanna retrieved her apron from her duffle bag. Although the apron was ridiculously traditional, she liked the way it accented her hourglass figure by making her waist appear even thinner. She placed the apron around her midsection and turned her back to Crystal. "Would you tie my apron?"

"Of course." As Crystal was tying the apron into a pleasing bow, she said, "How are you feeling today? Should I be on the lookout?"

Joanna looked back over her shoulder. "Yes, I think so. Yesterday, I hiked the long trail that goes through the meadow. It was beautiful. The little forest sunflowers had taken over the field, creating a sea of swishing yellow. It smelled fantastic and teemed with life." She smiled at the memory. "I mean, there were butterflies and so many bees roaming from one flower to the next, all doing their thing. And the little crickets hopped in and out of the grass while chirping away. For a bit, it transported me to another world, and I hardly noticed the exercise I was getting. That really lent itself to getting a good night's sleep."

"Okay, I got your back," said Crystal.

"Thanks, we'll see what happens."

After stowing their items in small lockers, the two women exited the break room to begin their shift. The peak of dinner customers came as usual. The tables filling as soon as they were empty, other servers bustling around, and when the serving window got full of hot dinners, Gus calling out, "Orders up."

Lucinda, the junior reporter who worked for the newspaper in town, appeared at the diner again. She chose a booth in Joanna's section and looked over the menu. Her body was thin with a long face to match, and she pinned her brown hair above her head, giving it a unique tussled look.

Joanna smiled and approached the table. "Hi Lucinda. I'm glad to see you again. You left in a hurry the other night."

"Hi Joanna. Oh, it was nothing. I thought I had a lead on a story, but not much happens in the town of Lightmeadow." Lucinda formed a wry smile. "I wish I could land a breakout story. Something exciting, you know?"

"I know what you mean. But most folks around here are happy that the biggest thing that goes on is when the high school boys knock over a bunch of mailboxes." Joanna picked up the menu from the table. When her eyes connected with Lucinda's, they shared a light laugh.

Lucinda nodded her head a couple of times. "I suppose you're right. Maybe I should see if the paper will let me write a story about something going on in Helinas." They both laughed some more. Joanna took her order and left to take care of other tables.

A man wearing jeans that had molded to the shape of his body, equally worn hiking boots, and a rugged short-sleeved shirt approached a booth in her section. He slid into the seat and placed his backpack next to him.

When Joanna went to the table, she thought he looked familiar. "Hi, can I get you something to drink?" she asked the man.

"I'll stick with water, thanks. Need to stay hydrated." He casually leaned back in the booth and looked at her with a grin. His straight blondish hair fell in front of one eye, and he used his hand to smooth it back in place.

"This is such a cliché, but have you been here before? You look familiar."

He shifted and rubbed his chin. "Yes, I stop in on my way to Balmar Cascades. I'm a photographer and sometimes I volunteer for the park system."

"Glad you're here with us again. We get a lot of regulars. I'm Joanna and I'll be waiting on you today."

He leaned across the table and offered her a handshake. "Hi Joanna. I'm Ratlin."

Joanna accepted his light grip on her fingers and produced a girlish smile. "Well, Ratlin. I'll be back to take your order."

When Joanna walked away, she couldn't help but glance over her shoulder to see Ratlin reading the menu. She continued to a nearby table and slid a tip from the last customer into her apron pocket before clearing the remaining dishes. When she got a moment, she flipped to the back of her pad and wrote Ratlin's name next to a brief description. Customers liked it when you remembered their name and something about them so, she got in the habit of making a note every time she met someone new.

What appeared to be two parents with a teen daughter piled into the only open booth Joanna had left. It took her multiple stops before she got to the small family. She noticed the father had neatly cut white hair, and the mother also had a short stylish cut that was accentuated by her flawless makeup. Joanna wondered how she looked so polished while traveling. The daughter had small headphones on and was bopping her head back and forth while looking at the menu.

"Thanks for waiting. How's everyone doing?" Joanna asked.

"We're fine," the father said in a slight mumble. He looked up from the menu and scanned the tables. "Looks like you do well here."

"Yes, we've had a busy day, but it's slowing down now." Joanna mimicked the man's behavior by looking around the room. "Are you ready to order or would you like to start with something to drink?"

"We'll order," the man said.

Joanna took his and his wife's order. She turned to the girl, who lowered the menu. Joanna felt the familiar sensation of the world starting to disappear around the young girl but shook it off. The girl pulled a headphone off one ear. "I'm going to have the chicken salad sandwich, but can I get it with fries instead of chips? Oh yah, and a chocolate shake."

"Sure." Joanna finished writing the order and continued circulating through her section. She got a little off beat because the young girl was on her mind, so she stopped at the cashier counter, which was at an angle where she could get a good look at her. This time she let the world disappear long enough so she could see inside her body and where the illness was located, then pulled back. It was a dark blotch that looked like it was on her heart. The darkness wasn't very large, but its edges were blurry, indicating to Joanna it was an infection.

Joanna had orders up and went to the pickup window. Crystal was there sharing a quick laugh with Gus while she gathered her plates full of hot food. Joanna gave Crystal a look, and the two paused past the window before taking out the orders.

"What's up?" Crystal asked.

"See the teenage girl in my section with the long, dark hair?" Joanna gestured her head in the teenager's direction.

"Really? The tall one? She's so young and looks so healthy."

"Yes, but it seems there's a problem with her heart." Joanna felt tension in her throat.

"Her heart? That's so sad. Can't you do something about it?"

"I'm not sure why, but I don't normally heal someone that young."

"I guess, I get it, but seems to me, since she is so young would be a good reason to do it. My brother was the same age when you helped him." Crystal shifted her weight onto her other hip and the plates of food in her hands moved in rhythm. "I mean, not only did he get better from his illness, but he grew somehow. Now he's the healthiest and happiest I've ever seen him. That's for sure."

Joanna looked at the ground trying to identify the intermingled feelings of resistance until she returned eye contact with Crystal. "Anyway, I don't know if we can pull this one off. She's sitting with her parents and there's still a bunch of people here." Contemplating a moment longer, she said, "I just put in their orders so, let's wait and see how it goes."

"All right," Crystal said.

The two of them quickly parted to get the food on the tables. It wasn't long before the family's order was ready, and Joanna took everything over to them. The parents seemed quiet, almost sullen. She made some small talk. "So, are you folks traveling through? Many people on the road stop here."

The father looked at her without a word, before the wife said, "Yes, we're headed to Helinas. We have a family member in the hospital there."

"Oh, I'm sorry to hear that. Please, let me know if there is anything else I can get for you. Anything at all." Joanna allowed a brief silence to pass while running her hands down the sides of her apron before leaving the table.

Joanna kept an eye on the family while she started cleaning and filling the condiments at the tables. Crystal came by with a box of sugar packets to fill the sugar caddies. Suddenly, the mother got up and inspected items in the small gift shop and the father followed her until he disappeared into the adjoining restroom. The daughter stayed at the table and returned her headphones over her ears.

Joanna looked at Crystal. Crystal turned her head and surveyed the family, then nodded before heading to the booth where the daughter was sitting and cleared the remaining dishes. The music still absorbed the girl into her own world, so Crystal sat the dishes on a nearby table and stalled there for a minute.

Joanna had already shifted positions, and the world around the girl had disappeared. Joanna's mind squeezed the blotch on the girl's heart. As she continued to squeeze the illness, her body grew warm, and love filled her insides. The energy released, and in a flash, it was done.

Joanna was regaining her bearings while Crystal checked on the girl.

The girl pulled one headphone away from her ear and looked at Crystal. Then she put a hand on her chest and said, "Whoa. I just had a moment."

"Really? What was that?" Crystal pulled out a rag and wiped off the table.

"I don't know. I was into this song, and it made me think of my grandmother. She's really sick. Then it was like someone prodded my heart and I got a little tingly inside, and my mind went completely blank." The girl rubbed her chest. "That was weird."

"Well, grandmothers have a way of pulling at our heartstrings."

"Yah, I guess so. We haven't been all that close lately, but I remember her being around a lot when I was little." The girl paused. "Traveling with my parents is so-o-o boring, but I'm glad I'm going to visit her."

"That sounds like a good idea. Can I get you anything else before you go?" Crystal asked.

"No, thanks. And it looks like my parents are waiting for me." The girl got up from the booth and the family disappeared out the door.

Joanna noticed Lucinda had her notepad out. After finishing what she was writing, Lucinda trailed out the door after the family. Crystal came closer to Joanna's side and as they watched the door close, Joanna said, "Lucinda has been here a lot lately. Do you think she's on to us?"

"Oh, I wouldn't worry. It's probably coincidence."

"All the same, maybe I should lie low for a while. Just in case," Joanna said.

"I guess. Lucinda might a journalist, but I can't imagine how she would figure anything out, really." Crystal slightly rolled her eyes.

A Steak That Big

ZOEY FOLLOWED HER PARENTS, Mitchell and Cathleen, out of the diner. As she got into the backseat of the oversized four-door Buick, she rubbed her chest because it still had a slight tingle inside. Once on the road, she pulled off her headphones and leaned closer to the front seat. "Mom?"

"Yes, honey."

"Do you ever feel love in your heart?"

"Well, sure. That's how you know it's love."

"No, no. I mean, like something is actually touching your heart? And like this sense of, I don't know, peace of mind."

"Well, yes. I think I know what you mean. I feel like that when I look at your father." Cathleen brushed the side of Mitchell's hair. Her father didn't take his eyes off the road, but tilted his head to rub it against her hand. Her mother turned back to Zoey. "And the day you were born. Oh, my. My entire chest was full of love and warmth." She hesitated. "Why are you asking about this?"

Zoey slid back in her seat and shrugged. "I was thinking about Grandma and felt something inside my chest."

"Well, your grandmother took care of you a lot when you were little. Dad and I were working full time, and she came to stay with us. You may have been too young to remember."

"I don't remember specific things really, more like I remember her being around a lot. And that she was funny. She made me laugh." Zoey grew a broad smile.

Her mother moved her eyes up and to the side before saying, "Yes, I guess you're right. You were a happy child, but Grandma always had you giggling and laughing." She turned to Mitchell. "What game did they always like to play?"

Her father adjusted in his seat. Then he glanced back to check for traffic before flicking the blinker and sliding the car into the right lane. "I don't remember any specific games, but Grandma would blow bubbles in the house and Zoey would have a blast running around trying to pop them all."

"Oh yes, she was always doing fun things like that." Her mother's smile shifted downward, and her eyes lost a little spark. "Maybe it's that Grandma is in hospice care. You're going to visit her and it's bringing up a lot of emotion. Sometimes, that happens when you realize someone you love won't always be a part of our lives."

Zoey tightened her lips. She thought about how she hadn't been close to anyone who died. Her Uncle Rudy passed away last year, and they attended the funeral, but she only met him a handful of times.

"Don't worry. It will be okay." Her mother gave a comforting smile.

Zoey looked out the window and listened to her parents' conversation for a couple of miles.

"About how long do we have to go?" Cathleen asked.

"About forty-five minutes, maybe an hour," Mitchell said.

"Is there going to be anyone staying at the house?"

"I think Erica and Rob and their family are coming next week. I figure if they do, we can grab a couple of hotel rooms closer to the hospital. The house would be pretty cramped." Mitchell let out a hearty breath. "We'll see how everything goes, but that would work out well. We'll just tell them we're getting a room for a night before going home. Then I can give Erica an update at the hospital, and we'll leave so they can have their own time to visit with Mom."

Zoey put her headphones back on and arranged a pillow to lean against the corner between the seat and window. After three or four songs, she dozed off and when she opened her eyes, they were on the highway traveling through the city, about to take the exit to her grandmother's house.

ZOEY AND HER PARENTS rode up the elevator at the hospital in silence. They reached the floor and walked into the hospice wing. Just inside the entrance was a small waiting room. Zoey and her mother stayed there so her father could visit with Grandma first. After a long half an hour, he returned to say that Grandma was doing well and excited to visit with them too, so he led them to where she was staying.

It was a comforting room, with drapes on the windows and a bedspread to match, but it didn't let you forget it was a hospital. The walls were stark white, and the smell of harsh disinfectants mingled with illness swirled around in the ventilated air. The sun shone into the room, and Grandma was sitting in a cushioned chair with a blanket covering her lap and midsection. Her face erupted in an enormous smile, and she stuck out her hands. "Oh, it's so good to see you. Come and give me a hug."

Her mother walked over to her first and leaned over to exchange a long hug. "Hello, Mom. So good to see you."

As soon as the hug ended, Grandma turned her attention to Zoey. "My darling! You've grown into a beautiful young woman."

Warmth rose in Zoey's cheeks as she returned her grandmother's warm embrace. "Thanks Grandma. It has been a while since I've seen you."

Everyone continued chatting as they found places to settle in the room. Zoey and her mother arranged chairs around Grandma and her father leaned on the edge of the bed. No one asked about Grandma's health or most recent prognosis. They jumped from topic-to-topic, catching up on life events small and large. Their last vacation that Cathleen adored, Zoey's upcoming graduation from high school, and Mitchell's latest promotion. Grandma told a story about when Grandpa got a big promotion at the furniture store, and they went to one of the fanciest restaurants in town to celebrate.

Zoey listened to every word, taking in the wrinkles on Grandma's face and how they moved with her facial expressions. Then suddenly, the room around Grandma seemed to disappear. It was as if the window and room around Grandma's silhouette got blurry. It made Zoey's head spin.

Zoey took a deep breath and refocused. Grandma was saying something about how she couldn't believe anyone would eat a steak that big when it happened again. The room faded and now Zoey was looking at

Grandma's chest and torso. Her body turned to fuzzy shades of white, grey, and black. Lots of black.

Fear zipped through Zoey as she asked herself what was happening. A wave of lightheadedness took over that was so strong it caused her to lean to the side and she almost lost balance. "Oh-oh," she said as she caught herself by grabbing an arm of the chair.

Grandma stopped talking, and when Zoey looked around at everyone, they were staring at her. With her eyes glassy and wide, she propped her head with one hand. "I must've gotten a little lightheaded."

Ready to get out of her chair, her mother asked, "My goodness. Are you okay?"

"Yes, I'm okay. I feel better now," Zoey replied.

"Did you have anything to eat at the house this morning? Are you hungry?" her mother probed.

"You know, maybe that's it. I didn't have much to eat." Zoey sat straight and got reoriented. "It's probably a good idea if I go down to the cafeteria and get something."

"Don't you want me to come with you?" Her mother was relentless.

"No, no. I'm okay. Stay here and visit with Grandma."

Cathleen put out her hand in Mitchell's direction. Mitchell knew what his wife wanted and placed some cash in Cathleen's open palm. Her mother handed the money to Zoey. "Here, get yourself something good to eat. And don't just pick at the outsides."

Zoey hid her irritation with her mother's comment and said, "Yah, sure. I can't wait to get something to eat." But what she really couldn't wait to do was to get out of the room. She slid the money into her pocket and headed for the door.

As she rounded the corner, she heard her father's voice. "Don't worry, Cathleen. She'll be fine. She just needs a break and to get something to eat."

Zoey wasted no time and got herself into the elevator, still wondering what had happened. One side of her mind examined how she felt for the moment when the world disappeared around her grandmother. She didn't have any thoughts in a way that reminded her of the peace of mind she experienced at the diner. It was soothing to have her mind be so silent. At the same time, the other side of her mind worked to convince herself that her mother was right, she needed to get some food in her stomach.

In the cafeteria, Zoey moved through the food line. She didn't notice the change, but she passed by some of her favorite foods, including crispy French fries. Instead, she settled on a fresh salad and balsamic dressing. As a last touch, she grabbed a two pack of oatmeal cookies, thinking that she needed a burst of sugar. After getting settled at a table where she could look out at the hospital courtyard, she took her time and ate until she was full.

ZOEY TOOK ONE STEP off the elevator on the hospice floor and a nurse was pushing an older woman in a wheelchair. They came closer and closer. She couldn't stop staring at the patient, who was smiling and looking up at her, anticipating a greeting. The world started to disappear and close in around the woman. Unsure what to do, Zoey nodded and diverted to the wing opposite from hospice. As she navigated the change in direction, she stumbled and almost bumped into the wheelchair. She mumbled, "So sorry."

"It's okay, dear," the patient replied, but Zoey was already walking at a quick pace down the hall.

There was no time to process the "Children's Oncology" sign as Zoey pushed through the huge double doors, looking for a place to escape. The doors closed behind her and she heard children playing nearby. The large nurse's station in front of her was empty, so she paused and looked around. Drawn to the sounds of children she let herself wander to the playroom around the corner. Once she peered through a viewing window, she stood and watched the children. Without knowing what was happening, the world around the children disappeared and their insides became transparent. This time she could make out the fuzzy outlines of bones and organs in white and grey without getting lightheaded.

Then there was the blackness. The illness. There was a cute boy with shining eyes who had splotches of blackness streaking through the insides of his bones. On the other side of the room there were two younger girls smiling and playing with oversized blocks who had a diffused blackness that appeared in their neck, radiated around to their underarms, and on one of them it vaguely reappeared on her stomach. Zoey developed an intense compassion for the children, alongside a deep admiration for their resilience. Although they had to feel sick from their illness and the side effects of their treatment, these children were still finding joy in what they were doing.

What seemed like a force stronger than her pulled her to the doorway. Her steps remained soft, and she moved slowly. She placed a hand on the doorframe and peered into the room. Inside the threshold, another little girl was playing with a doll. Both the little girl and the doll had soft brown wavy hair and chubby cheeks. Zoey focused on the girl so she could see inside her body. On the side of the girl's brain was a clear black splotch with fine tendrils gripping down into the crevices.

The little girl startled Zoey when she said, "Hi. My name is Jessica. Do you want to play dolls with me?" The little girl smiled and extended a doll in Zoey's direction.

"No, I don't think so," Zoey managed to say.

With a distinct pout, the little girl brought the doll back closer and continued playing with the cluster of toys within her reach. Even though Jessica's pout had faded, it brought Zoey back to experiencing a deep compassion. The compassion grew, and she stared at the black splotch on Jessica's brain. Something activated in a part of her mind she didn't know existed.

In the complete silence, Zoey's mind pulled the creeping tendrils back into the splotch, then squeezed the darkness. Her compassion elevated into warmth and an escalating love as her mind continued to squeeze harder. The love itself grew until it was an intensity that she never imagined was possible. Her mind squeezed the splotch harder and harder. With no one to guide her on how to make a smooth release, the energy built until her chest felt it would burst, and it pushed upwards, creating pressure against her eardrums that made a painful rushing sound.

Finally, the release came, and Zoey's head snapped back. Her ears rang with a pitch that penetrated to the insides of her brain. Feeling nauseated, she leaned forward and covered her ears with her hands, but that only amplified the sound. The room dimmed around her for a couple of seconds, and she fell against the door frame. Her hands grasped whatever she could to maintain balance while her awareness returned to normal. It was like waking up from a bad dream, but it wasn't over yet.

Can't You See It?

ZOEY COULD HEAR JESSICA crying and saw two nurses running down the hallway in her direction. The other children in the playroom had become frozen in place, transformed into statues staring at Jessica. A male nurse was the first to arrive at the playroom, and he pushed Zoey to the side. He slowed his actions and squatted down close to the girl, who was still crying out loud, tears streaming down her chubby cheeks. The male nurse calmly asked, "Jessica, what happened? Are you okay?"

Jessica looked around the room. "I don't know." She cried again, then sucked in her breath with a sniffle. "Something poked me. It poked me inside my head and now it feels funny." She let a few more tears fall and rubbed her head in the same area where the splotch appeared to Zoey.

A female nurse had also arrived and was standing behind Zoey. The nurse tugged her shoulder, so it forced her to turn and look at her. The female nurse bluntly asked, "Who are you? What happened?" Her forehead furrowed, and she placed a hand on each hip.

"I… I…" stammered Zoey. Now her eyes were filling with tears.

"Are you a close relative?"

"No. I just…"

The female nurse looked at the male nurse and said, "We noticed her on the camera, but she looked older. We thought she was a parent." She turned again to Zoey and raised her voice, "What the hell happened?"

Zoey turned her attention to the playroom. The male nurse continued to comfort Jessica, and the other children remained silent. "I just. You don't understand."

"Explain it to me," the nurse said.

"They're all sick. All of them. Can't you see it?" Panic rose into Zoey's chest, threatening to take her over.

"Well, yes, they're sick. That's why they are here." The female nurse continued to stare at Zoey and finally softened her expression. "It can be upsetting. No one expects children to be in an oncology unit. It's not fair, but it happens. Even the clinicians here have hard days."

"But can't you see it? You're a nurse. I would think out of all people, you could see it too. Can't you see the illness streaking inside his bones?" Zoey waved a hand in the little boy's direction.

The female nurse returned her hands to her hips. "How do you know that?" Silence flowed through the tension in the air. She escalated her tone. "I asked, how do you know that?"

The male nurse stood and quietly said, "Kayla, why don't you two have this conversation somewhere else?"

The two women pivoted their heads to face the male nurse. Kayla let out a breath and replied, "Yes, of course. You're right. We'll go down to the waiting room and have a chat." Kayla led the way down the hall to the waiting room and stood by the doorway.

Zoey walked into the room and chose a seat, not sure what to expect. A box of tissues was sitting on the side table, and she grabbed a couple to dab her eyes. She said things in the hallway that may seem so out of sight she should have kept them to herself. It would be better to back-up and agree her behavior was an emotional reaction to seeing the children, but she would have to keep in mind they had her on camera.

The nurse disappeared for a moment and returned with a bottle of water that she handed to Zoey. "Here, a drink of water will help. Now, let's start the conversation over." The nurse sat down across from Zoey, leaned forward, and rested her folded hands between her knees. "As you probably heard, my name is Kayla. I'm a nurse in the hospital and have been here for almost nine years now."

Zoey took a drink of water. "I'm Zoey. I'm here visiting my grandmother in the hospice wing. Sorry, this is my first time in the hospital, and I got a little lost." She bounced her knee. "You're right. It upset me to find all the children here. I figured the boy was on some type of chemo treatment because he doesn't have any hair." She looked down and played with the edges of the label on the water bottle. When Zoey looked up, Kayla was waiting for her eye contact.

"I see." Kayla let out a breath. "And what about the little girl? What happened that made her cry?"

"She asked me to play dolls with her, and I said no, that I couldn't. Then she turned away and started crying." Zoey swallowed the last of the moisture in her mouth. "I was so surprised she started crying that when I tried to step back, I lost my balance and fell against the doorway. After that, you and the other nurse were coming down the hallway."

"Okay."

"I didn't mean to make her cry. This has been a terrible day." Zoey looked at the ceiling for a few seconds. "My mother can tell you. I've been having a hard time with my emotions and everything, especially being here to visit my grandmother."

The male nurse appeared in the doorway. "Hi, how is everything going?"

Kayla turned in his direction. "This is Zoey. We're finishing our conversation and I'm going to walk with her to find her mother."

The male nurse pivoted to the side. "All right. Let me know if you need anything. I'll be at the nurse's station."

Kayla returned her attention to Zoey. "Are you ready?"

"Yes, I think so." Zoey stood up and left the oncology unit with Kayla.

"My grandmother's room is down on the left side," Zoey said.

"Why don't you wave for your mom to come into the hallway? That would probably be the least disruptive," Kayla said.

"Um yah, okay."

"That way you can go in and visit with your grandmother while your mother and I have a quick talk."

Zoey said nothing in reply. The private conversation between adults just added to her distress over everything that had happened. She followed the nurse's wishes, and her mother came out into the hall-way.

Impatient to move things forward, Kayla stepped closer and introduced herself. "May I talk with you for a moment?"

Cathleen paused before saying, "Yes, of course. What is this concerning?"

Zoey sensed Kayla's stare. "I'm going to go and visit with Grandma." She left the two women, hoping for the best.

Inside the room, she found that Grandma was the only person there and asked, "Where did Dad go?"

"It was his turn to get something to eat. Come sit with me. Are you feeling better?" Grandma said with a growing smile.

Zoey sat in the chair next to her. "I guess. It's been a really weird couple of days, Grandma."

"Oh, darling." She leaned towards Zoey and put her hand on her shoulder. "It will get better. I promise."

"Promise?"

"Yes, absolutely." Her grandmother nodded. "Now tell me, what else is going on in your life? Who are your friends? What do you like to do for fun?"

Zoey chatted back and forth with Grandma. At first, Zoey avoided looking at her until she figured out that if she focused on the moment and on being centered deep inside, nothing happened. It even helped to sit straight-up. The world around her stayed in place and she didn't transition to seeing inside Grandma's body. Rather, she relaxed and enjoyed the visit.

The spell was broken when her mother walked into the room with concern spread across her face. She sat in the chair opposite from Grandma and produced a meager smile. "What are you guys talking about?"

"Zoey was telling me about all her favorite music," said Grandma.

"That sounds nice. Goodness knows she is always wearing her headphones," replied her mother. They all shared a laugh and Zoey blushed a little.

IN THE HALLWAY, ZOEY and her mother made their way to the elevator. The silence remained until they stepped out of the open doors.

"I'm supposed to meet your father in the atrium." Her mother scanned the area. "The sitting area looks lovely. Why don't you wait there while I go find him?"

"Yah, okay," Zoey replied. She wondered if her banishment to the sitting area was because her mother wanted a chance to talk with her father alone. Certainly, what happened with the nurse wouldn't be forgotten. Going with the flow, Zoey settled into one of the larger chairs. She wished she had brought her mp3 player and headphones along. It didn't seem right tuning out when she visited Grandma, but she missed having it for times like these. Just sitting, waiting, alone with her thoughts. This time, the events from the day were spinning through her mind.

A woman dressed in business attire walked over and in one motion sat down in the seat next to Zoey while releasing an exaggerated sigh of relief.

After the sigh ended, the woman twisted her head to meet eyes with Zoey. "Hello, my name is Lucinda Ambriel and I'm a reporter from Lightmeadow. I'm working on a piece about spontaneous healing."

Zoey glanced at the reporter, then let her eyes examine the atrium.

Undeterred, the woman kept staring at Zoey. "I was wondering if you would answer a few questions about your visit to the hospital today." She leaned forward, still attempting to make a connection.

"Forget it lady, I'm only a teenager," Zoey said.

Lucinda pulled a card from the inside pocket of her jacket. "Well, here's my card. If you change your mind, all we need is your parents' permission. It wouldn't take long."

Zoey snatched the card and read it over. "Lightmeadow, that sounds familiar, but it's not around here." She pulled her eyebrows together and looked at Lucinda.

"No, it's north of here. Where the diner is located."

"The diner?"

"Yes, the Wayside Retreat Diner. Many people driving through stop there." Lucinda continued her fishing expedition.

"Oh, the nice restaurant with cool wallpaper and stuff but regular diner food."

"You have been there?"

"Yah, I guess so." Zoey crossed her arms again with the card still in her hand. "What does that have to do with anything?"

"Did anything happen to you when you were there?"

"Happen to me? What are you talking about?"

"Anything strange? Out of the ordinary?"

Zoey remembered the events at the diner, including the tingling sensation in her heart and peace of mind, but pushed the memories aside. "You're crazy lady. Go find someone else to bother." Zoey's attempt to push away the memories from the diner only allowed the events from during the day to resurface. A lump formed in her throat, and her eyes stung. She looked away from the woman. In her new line of vision, her mother was walking towards her with a look of determination only a mother could possess when they sense something is awry around their child. "Don't look now, here comes my mother."

Lucinda stayed steady. "Oh good. I would like to meet her." She stood-up and extended a hand to Zoey's mother. "Hello, I'm Lucinda Ambriel, a reporter from Lightmeadow."

"A reporter? My daughter is a minor. You shouldn't be talking to her and actually, I don't care who you are, you leave her alone," said Cathleen.

"Oh. I was just wondering if…" Lucinda pulled her hand back and moved it in Zoey's direction.

"I don't care what you are wondering. What is wrong with you? Who asks people questions in a hospital?" Cathleen interjected.

"I'm working on a piece about spontaneous healing."

"Well, you know what? We're here visiting a loved one in hospice care. Go see if you can heal them." Her mother leaned across Lucinda and waved Zoey out of her chair. "Let's go. Your father's going to grab a cab later."

Please Help Us

THERE WAS MORE SILENCE in the car. Zoey looked out the side window and tried to concentrate on the scenery. Once they were in the flow of traffic on the highway, her mother gave her a glance.

"So, do you want to tell me what happened today?" she asked.

"I don't know. I guess everything is a bit much." Zoey shrugged.

"The nurse said you got lost and ended up in children's oncology. She said you got overwhelmed by the thoughts that the children are ill."

"Yah, I guess so. They are so young and everything. I hate to be like this, but Grandma is old. We expect her to become sick but those young kids..." The hum of the tires rolling along the highway took over the inside of the car until Zoey continued, "But they were playing and still having fun. They're so resilient. It's uplifting and heartbreaking at the same time."

"Yes, they deserve to be children, protected from the world and free from worries." Her mother allowed a space in the conversation. "The nurse also said she was concerned because you talked like you could see their illness with your eyes."

Zoey knew it wasn't a good idea to explain everything to her mother, so she stuck with the story she told Kayla. "Oh, I was just upset by everything. One little boy didn't have any hair, and I figured it was from his treatment. You could see that everything wasn't okay."

"Try not to let everything overwhelm you." Her mother checked the car mirrors before making a lane change. "Your father and I raised you to be grounded in scientific ways of thinking and not fall into the labyrinth of religion based purely on beliefs." She sighed. "But maybe it would have been better to provide some kind of spiritual practice."

Zoey critically examined her mother's silhouette. "I guess I hadn't thought about it much."

"Well, many of us don't until we are forced to, but the truth is, no one really knows what happens after we die. It maybe the end, but it may also be a new beginning. I rest assured that there is something more beyond this world and you should, too." Her mother gave Zoey a side glance while keeping both hands on the steering wheel.

"I'm not sure why, but I'm liking that way of looking at things. It seems natural or something," Zoey said.

"Good, I'm glad. And I'm glad we had some time to talk, just the two of us." Her mother kept her focus on the road and clumsily patted Zoey's arm.

As soon as Zoey and her mother finished with dinner, Zoey left the kitchen to find solitude in a hot shower. The shower lasted so long a fog filled the bathroom. The tiny water droplets met her when she pulled back the shower curtain. Then they swirled around her legs and feet as she stepped onto the rug before quickly dissolving in the drafty house.

When Zoey reached the living room, her mother was sitting on the couch. Her mother stretched her neck and leaned forward to look at her across the room.

"Let's watch a movie." Her mother smiled. "Your father got here not too long ago. He's upstairs. It's no surprise, but he wanted to read before bed. He probably has his nose in some technical paper or biology journal."

"Yah, sure," Zoey replied.

After a few steps to the couch, Zoey was next to her grandmother's upright piano. She ran her hands over the smooth wood of the fall board that covered the keys. Her fingers roamed lower to lift the cover and expose the keys, lovingly worn from many years of use. She slid her fingers across the keys until she pressed down the white key closest to the middle. The piano responded by sending the middle C note into her ears. The smell of Grandma's rose scented soap from the shower floated into her nose. Suddenly she heard Grandma hum in tune with the note in her mind. Zoey closed her eyes and relaxed into the pleasant childhood memory. She was sitting on the floor with a tiny toy piano. Grandma had kneeled on the ground next to her and gently talked in her ear. She whispered, "Okay, now hit this key."

Zoey pushed the key, and the piano produced a note that sounded like a muffled ring of a bell. Grandma echoed the sound with her hum again and said, "Now you try." She leaned around Zoey and pressed the key.

Shyness struck Zoey, and she looked at Grandma, who nodded and repeated the process. They worked through three more keys, the piano creating distinct notes and Zoey humming to mimic the sound. Finally, she burst out in laughter and fell on her side. Grandma squeezed her shoulder and said, "We can work on this more later."

The memory left as quickly as it came, but a distinct feeling lingered. Back in the moment, Zoey took in the piano keys with her eyes and closed the fall board. "Mom?"

Her mother turned to Zoey with a curious look. "Yes, honey."

"Can I take some piano lessons?" Zoey asked.

"Piano? You haven't talked about playing piano before."

"I know, but you know how I like my music. I was thinking it would be a good idea to take up an instrument. Maybe try piano."

"Well, sure. If you still want to take some lessons when we get home, we'll talk to your father and make the arrangements. I think it's a great idea," her mother said.

"Okay." Zoey plopped onto the couch next to her mother.

IN THE DARK OF night, Zoey got settled into the guestroom on the first floor. The bed had an old single mattress with a thin flower bedspread. But there were two fluffy pillows that helped to make everything feel cozy. It took her some time to get to sleep after such a strange day and spending another night in a strange bedroom.

It didn't take long before her deep sleep became invaded by dreams. The sound of the toy piano surrounded her, but the notes took on an angelic tone. Zoey was running her hands over the keys of a piano, when suddenly she was in Grandma's hospital room. Grandma was there and the sunlight coming in the window surrounded her like a glowing halo.

"Zoey, darling," she said and put out her arms. "There is nothing to be afraid of, nothing to worry about."

Zoey eagerly walked towards her grandmother. She fell into her arms and Grandma enclosed her in a comforting embrace. Everything went dark, and the scene shifted to being in the hospital hallway.

Wind was flowing down the hall, sending a chill up Zoey's body to the tops of her arms. The air had a hazy quality, and the white walls and ceiling were tinted with a dingy grey. Patients in their hospital gowns started coming out of rooms along the hall from every direction. Some appeared while moving along in wheelchairs. The patients were smiling and looked bright, but as they drew closer, they became dull, and took on the grey tones that surrounded them. They started mumbling things Zoey didn't understand. With each step, the skin on their faces got more and more sickly, and the rings around their eyes became darker. A stench rose in the air, the stench only illness creates.

She wasn't sure how many patients had appeared, but they were all slowly closing in around her. Her chest tightened, and an intense fear took hold of her from the inside out.

Still becoming sicklier, some patients limped or struggled to roll their wheelchair, but they kept drawing closer in every direction. The mumbling became distinct, and she could make out some phrases. "Save us," they said.

Zoey turned her head in another direction. "Please help us," some of them said.

Her gaze darted to the other side of her where other patients said, "Heal us."

They moved in closer and in their last steps before reaching Zoey, they started chanting in unison, *Save us. Please help us. Heal us.* The chant came over and over as the stench of illness intensified. *Save us. Please help us. Heal us.*

Just as one patient reached out to touch Zoey, she woke up, let out an overwrought scream and sat up in bed.

With fear coursing through her entire being, she wondered where she was, and her eyes strained until her brain adjusted to being awake. A hint of light from the oncoming sunrise made a small glow around the edges of the curtains that helped her to make out the dresser with a lamp sitting on top. She remembered she was at Grandma's house and heard footsteps coming down the stairs.

"Honey, was that you? What's the matter?" Her mother's voice traveled into the bedroom.

Zoey gathered herself and said, "I just had a bad dream. It's nothing. I'm fine."

Her mother had made it to the doorway and took a step into the room. "Are you sure?"

"Really, I'm fine. You can go back to bed."

"I suppose." Cathleen stared at her daughter and slowly turned to head back upstairs.

Zoey fell back onto the pillow and put a hand on her forehead. She focused on the increasing amount of sunlight sneaking into the room. The memories of the last couple of days moved through her mind, and she remembered Lucinda saying, "I'm doing a piece on spontaneous healing."

She focused her thoughts then remembered she had slid the reporter's business card in the back pocket of her jeans.

What a Night

THE PARKING LOT AT the diner was almost full when Joanna pulled in and found a spot away from the main entrance. The rain and drizzle must have encouraged drivers to take a break from the wet roads.

Dan, another server who was on since before lunch, spied her walking through the dining area. He looked at Joanna with pleading eyes, so she met him halfway through the diner.

"I'm so glad you're here." Dan shifted a tray of dishes in his hands. "Can you get started right away? We have been steady since lunch."

"Sure, give me a minute to get my apron on," Joanna said.

Gus made a call for orders up, and Dan hurried on his way.

Joanna dove into her shift and was busy enough that she wasn't sure when Crystal arrived. The dinner rush was in full swing. She spied Ratlin sliding into one of her booths. Before she gathered her orders from the serving window, she flipped to the back of her pad and refreshed her memory about the first time they met. Then she rotated through her section, eventually ending up where he was sitting.

"Hello Ratlin, good to see you again. What would you like today?" Joanna asked.

Ratlin grinned and his eyes flashed to Joanna's name tag. "Hi Joanna."

"That's no fair. You looked at my nametag." Joanna giggled.

He rubbed his chin, then slid back in the booth. "You caught me. What can I say?"

Joanna took his order and continued the conversation. "So, what do you do with your photography?"

"I sell stock photos and I just worked with a great writer to publish a travel book."

"Really? That's excellent. Is the book about the Balmar Cascades?"

"Yah, thanks. It's about the park waterfalls and the other sights on the hiking trails."

Joanna leaned over with her hand out, and Ratlin handed her his menu. "Gus would probably want to put some in the giftshop. Travel books about the area are hot sellers. You should bring copies with you next time."

Ratlin raised an eyebrow. "Absolutely. I will be sure of it. I may even have a copy in the truck for Gus to take a look at."

"That would be perfect." Joanna produced her girlish smile and swayed her shoulders side-to-side. It was almost impossible not to flirt with him a little.

"Order's up!" Gus's voice carried through the diner.

"Speaking of Gus." Joanna smiled. She stopped at the last table in her section before heading to the serving window where Crystal had gathered the plates for her tables.

"Travis is in my section." Crystal groaned. "I don't suppose you'll take him?" She took a few steps and looked back at Joanna with an exaggerated pout.

Joanna chided back. "He normally sits in my section. It's your turn for a change." She grabbed her orders and returned to working the floor. The traffic of customers slowed to a steady pace, and Joanna was preparing tables for the next round of hungry travelers when she heard her name. She looked up to see Ratlin approaching her with his book in hand.

"Here you go, a complimentary copy for the diner." He started paging through the book.

Joanna stepped closer to peer at the contents. "The pictures are wonderful." She pointed to one. "Oh, this waterfall is lovely. Is it the Majestic Cascade?"

"That one? Yah, it was close to sunset during the fall and the colors reflected off…" Ratlin jerked his head to look across the diner. He handed the book to Joanna in a slow handoff, and she followed his line of sight. With two long steps, he was close to the booth where Travis was sitting, and Crystal was standing with plates in each hand.

Joanna didn't see the entire interaction, but she caught Travis's hand on Crystal's hip in a deep squeeze. His hands were large enough that his thumb was on her hipbone and the tips of his fingers were mushing into the flesh of her plush behind.

Once Ratlin's presence entered the space, Travis dropped his hand. Joanna brought the book to her chest and instinctively hugged the meager barrier. She watched the rest of the interaction. Crystal quickly set the plates back on the table and headed her direction.

"Did you see that?" Crystal asked.

"Some of it. What happened?" Joanna said.

"I brought him dessert and cleared the table. Then he said something like, thanks honey, and what I thought was going to be a pat on my hip turned out to become a grab that included half my ass." Crystal crossed her arms tight. "He squeezed all that he could get in that palm of his and wasn't in any hurry to let go. I thought I would have to drop the dishes to shake him off." She shook her head. "I knew he was a creep."

The two women fell silent as they watched Ratlin talking with Travis. Ratlin looked casual and was using an elbow to lean on the back of the booth. He gestured towards the room, and, after a little more conversation, they both laughed.

"Who's that?" Crystal asked.

"That's Ratlin." Joanna filled Crystal in on what she knew about him.

"He's something." Crystal's voice was full of awe.

"He sure is."

"It was smooth. He just strolled up and said that you needed help with an order."

Joanna looked at Crystal. "Oh, really?"

"Uh huh. Then he said that the two of them were going to have a talk, man-to-man."

Joanna watched Ratlin wrapping up the conversation. "It never occurred to me until now but, it's probably hard for Travis, having lost his parents when he was so young and being brought up by his grandmother. He really didn't have a father figure." She hugged the book tighter. "Maybe that's why he acts the way he does sometimes."

"Well, I don't have that much empathy," Crystal said flatly.

Joanna opened the book just as Ratlin shifted away from the table. Crystal leaned in to see and they flipped through a few pages. Out of the corner of her eye, Joanna noticed Lucinda headed to a booth in her section.

"You like the book?" Ratlin asked.

"Yes, it's impressive," Joanna said.

Ratlin looked at Crystal. "And I don't believe I've met you yet."

"Hi. I'm Crystal. Thanks for what you did."

Ratlin bowed slightly in Crystal's direction. "You're welcome. Are you okay?"

Crystal twirled a stray curl of hair around her finger. "Yes, now I am."

"I'm glad." Ratlin locked eyes with Crystal and they stood motionless for a couple of heartbeats. He broke the trance by clearing his throat and looking at Joanna. "Next time I'll try to come when it's not so busy."

"That would be great," Joanna replied.

"It's good to have met you, Crystal." Ratlin locked eyes with her again. "I should get a move on."

Joanna and Crystal watched him until the door closed behind his exit. Crystal leaned her head back and fanned her face with her hand. They both laughed and returned to focus on their tables that had been neglected far too long.

Joanna took orders from two tables before ending up in front of Lucinda. Like a child caught doing something naughty, she felt her stomach tighten. "Hello Lucinda. Did you finally take a break from our food?"

"Sort of. I was out of town and met a couple of interesting people."

"That sounds fun. What can I get for you today?"

"I'm going to change the pace and have the large house salad with blue cheese dressing. I love blue cheese dressing. It's just so decadent."

Joanna wrote down the order. "But the dressing is good. Gus makes it from scratch. Anything else?"

"Well, now that you asked. How about you agree to an interview?"

"Me? I don't have anything interesting to say. I'm sure there are better people to interview."

"But I think you do have something interesting to tell. Something *very* interesting." Lucinda handed her menu to Joanna. "One of the people I met on my trip was a man, about forty-seven-years-old, and he recently recovered from cancer." Lucinda rested her hand on the side of her face. "Interesting, don't you think?"

"Yes, that sounds interesting," Joanna said.

"You know what's even more interesting?" Lucinda shifted and folded her hands on the table. "His doctors told him they had no explanation why his symptoms subsided, and the tumor disappeared. Of course, he didn't care so much about that part. He said he felt great."

"Wow, that's incredible. Good for him." Joanna said. The tightness in her stomach had turned into a sailor's knot. She worried she would throw up at any moment, right there in the middle of the diner.

"You know who I also met? A young girl at the hospital in Helinas. She was there with her parents visiting a sick relative."

Although there was no permanent getaway, Joanna was finished with the conversation. "That doesn't sound so interesting. It seems sad to me. Let me put this order in for you." She quickly pivoted and walked away from the table.

Joanna spied Crystal at the serving window and headed that direction. She almost bumped into a customer along the way, but she reached Crystal just in time and waved her over to their usual spot.

With twin plates balanced on both hands and arms, Crystal frowned at Joanna. "What? What is it?"

"It's Lucinda. She knows," Joanna said.

"Knows what? What are you talking about?"

"She knows about me."

"No, she doesn't. She may have suspicions, but she can't really put anything together," Crystal rebutted.

Despite the food in Crystal's balance, Joanna tugged her further to the side and spoke in a rapid whisper. "She said she talked to a young girl visiting a relative in the hospital at Helinas. Remember the family with the teenager who had a problem with her heart? That's exactly what the mother told me."

"That could just be a coincidence."

"She said she wants to interview me," Joanna rebutted this time.

"Okay, go back and see if you can find out more. Play her game. Don't let on and see what you can get from her," Crystal said.

"All right. I'll do my best."

"Shit, what a night." Crystal hustled to her tables.

The entire situation was distracting, but Joanna navigated her work with a smooth grace. It wasn't long before Lucinda's food was ready, and she took it over to the table.

"Thanks. So, what do you think?" asked Lucinda.

"Not much. I understand you want a big story, but there isn't anything I can tell you."

"Well, I guess I'll have to write the article without your input." Lucinda dribbled some blue cheese dressing on her salad. "Of course, there was also Crystal's brother, Brandon, who recovered from his heart condition. It was the talk of the town, his being so successful on the cross-country team and all."

Once again, Joanna had heard all she wanted to hear. She leaned over and placed one hand on her hip. "All right Lucinda. I'm at work. This isn't the appropriate time or place to be having such a conversation. Anyway, like I said, I don't have anything to tell you."

Lucinda closed her eyes tight and nodded her head. "Of course, you're right. I'll stop. If you change your mind, you know where to find me."

Joanna gave Lucinda an intense stare. "Just ask if you need anything else. I'll be back with the check."

THE LIGHTS OUTSIDE THE diner were dimmed, the doors locked for the night, and the last customers had left. Joanna was working with Crystal to clean and prep the tables for the following day. She told Crystal about the last conversation with Lucinda and that she mentioned Brandon.

Crystal stayed silent and focused on filling the salt shakers. She screwed a top on and set a shaker on the table with a distinct thump. "Well, I still think she doesn't have enough yet for a believable story."

"I'm not so sure. Anyway, she has enough that she tried to get me to do an interview." Joanna slid into a chair at the table. "When it was my grandmother and I it was different. Now I'm tired of hiding." She fiddled with the dishcloth in her hands. "All the sneaking around seems wrong. And if it was out in the open, maybe I could help other healers with their abilities. Maybe even bring healers together to form a society or something." Joanna looked at Crystal. "I couldn't imagine being a healer alone."

Crystal kept her eyes on her work. "I guess, I get it." She allowed a silence to pass. "But if the article were to happen, it could be bad. People in Lightmeadow don't like change, and they certainly don't like anything out of the ordinary."

"I know." Joanna got up and went back to completing her side work.

They finished for the night and Crystal stopped before walking out into the cool night air. "If you do the interview is totally up to you. And if Lucinda pursues the article on her own, and she approaches me for information, I wouldn't say a word. But if you do it and want me to have your back, then I will."

"Thanks. That means a lot to me. This has been such a crazy night. Let's get out of here." Joanna closed the door behind them.

Now I'm Thanking You

AFTER ONE STEP INSIDE, Joanna couldn't remember embracing the comfort of being home so much. She stopped and leaned against the door to breathe in the familiar smells as she rubbed her throbbing forehead. Her feet ached, too. She kicked off her shoes one at a time, so they thumped against the wall.

A familiar clinking sound ruminated from the kitchen. She followed the noise to find Sanders putting away the clean dishes. Standing at the kitchen doorway, she watched him put a serving platter on a top shelf and a small smile grew on her face. He turned and looked in her direction.

"Hey baby, I didn't hear you come in."

Joanna walked into the room and sat in a chair at the kitchen table. When the weight of her body transferred to the seat, she let out a soft groan. She propped her head on one hand and returned Sanders's gaze.

"Is everything okay?" He asked.

"Um-huh. Just a strange day."

"You want to talk about it?"

Joanna looked at Sanders deeply. She wasn't sure how he would react to the events that transpired with Lucinda. "Well, I'm not excited about it, but I think we should talk."

"It sounds like it might be something serious." His facial expression took a downward turn, and he stepped in Joanna's direction but allowed the kitchen island to stay in between them.

"I guess." Joanna played with the napkin holder on the table. "Apparently, Lucinda has been keeping an eye on things in the diner. She followed some customers who I helped to get better after they left. Now, she's convinced she has evidence of that and wants to interview me." Joanna sighed. "To make things a bit more complicated, she also said that she would write the story whether or not she gets my interview." Joanna looked back to Sanders.

The silence was abrupt. Sanders picked up a kitchen towel and wiped his hands. Without looking at her he said, "Not this again, Joanna."

Joanna's mouth stopped in mid-motion for a moment before saying, "I'm surprised that is your response after I helped your father and everything."

He tossed the towel abruptly to the side, and it slid part way down the counter. "That's just it. I believe you, but no one can say for sure how he got better. Even the doctors said they didn't know and sometimes it just happens. Sometimes people get better when all the odds are against it." He snorted. "Why is Lucinda even wasting her time?"

Joanna's entire body stiffened, and she stared at Sanders. Her lips had no words. She watched as he put both hands on the counter and looked at the floor.

When he looked at her again, his expression had softened, and he walked around the kitchen island and sat in the chair next to her. He leaned forward to smooth her hair behind her ear then cupped the side of her face. He looked her in the eyes and softly said, "I'm sorry. I got upset. Everything is going so well for us right now, and an article like Lucinda is suggesting would disrupt our lives."

Joanna averted his gaze and nodded her head. "I know."

"And I just started my new job and everything. It took years to get this far."

"Yes, of course."

"So, why don't you tell her there's no way she can prove anything and to leave you alone? To just leave *it* alone?"

Joanna put her fingers around Sander's wrist and gently pulled his hand away from her face. Her chair scraped against the floor as she slid away from the table. "I'm not sure how I'm going to handle everything yet. How about we talk more about this later?" She had posed it as a question but didn't wait for a reply before walking out of the kitchen. With a brief look over her shoulder, she said, "I'm going to get ready for bed." Her steps on the old stairs made a variety of creaking sounds that matched the emotions moving from her body into her thoughts.

SUNLIGHT FLOODED THE BEDROOM. Joanna smiled and stretched her arms and legs, preparing her to get out of bed. Sanders had opened the curtains before he left for work and the house was quiet, allowing her mind to recall the events from the previous day. In an attempt to ignore the queasy feeling returning to her stomach, she rolled over and stuffed her face into a pillow.

It took some inner encouragement for her to get out of bed, dressed, and ready for the day. By then her stomach had changed direction and was rumbling with hunger, so she headed for the kitchen. When her feet hit the landing, the doorbell rang.

Most everyone didn't use the doorbell. Heat flooded her body, and she clenched her jaw as she tightly clasped the doorhandle while thinking that it could be Lucinda, more than ready to bother her at home. She flung the door open and found Brandon standing on the porch.

"Hi Joanna. I'm sorry, is this a bad time?" Brandon took a small step back.

Joanna hung on to the door handle and put her free hand on her chest. "No, no, it's fine. I thought you were someone else." She opened the screen door. "Please, come in."

"I brought fresh pastries from Pauline's Bakery." He extended a small box in Joanna's direction.

"Oh, thank you." She accepted the box and brought her nose closer to embrace the cinnamon laced sweetness that hung in the air. "How did you know I'm starving?" She smiled and waved Brandon towards the kitchen.

Joanna made coffee while Brandon got comfortable at the table. They made idle conversation until there were plates of pastries in front of them and mugs of coffee in their hands.

"Well, Brandon. I have a good idea, but let's hear it. What brings you by this morning?" Joanna looked over her coffee mug as she took a sip.

"Yah, um. I talked to my sister last night, and I had to pry to get it out of her, but she told me what happened yesterday at the diner with Lucinda." He took a small bite of his pastry and rubbed his hands together. "I thought about it, and I wanted to say a few things that I've put off telling you." He met eyes with Joanna.

"Okay," Joanna said.

"Well, when I started to faint after long runs and I had to stop doing cross-country for six months, it was pretty terrible for me."

"I can only imagine."

"Sure. But when the doctors said it was that the muscles in my heart were too thick to pump enough blood through my body, I forget what they called it, HCM or something…" He trailed off and took a drink of coffee. "That was another blow. No one wants to have heart surgery and be on medication for the rest of their life when they're seventeen."

"Yes, I remember."

"Then you helped me." He gestured his hands in Joanna's direction. "When you did what you did, I felt it. I felt what I can only describe as a warmth in my heart that spread throughout my chest. It was pretty amazing." He shyly laughed and developed a blush. "The other thing that happened was my mind became so silent, it was at peace. After that, it left something else inside of me, a completeness that never left. It really changed me in more ways than one."

Brandon went back to taking a few bites of pastry. "As you know, I got better, and the doctors said my echocardiogram was completely normal, but they didn't have a medical explanation for how I got better. They said I must have grown out of it." He let out a hearty laugh this time and leaned forward. "Grew out of it. How ridiculous."

Joanna laughed with him but kept eye contact so she could take in what was on Brandon's mind.

"After that, of course, I returned to cross-country. But I also started going to the art museum." His blush returned, and he looked to the side. "I used to love going as a kid. My mother took me all the time." He smiled. "From there, I started drawing and taking classes. Next thing I knew, I was doing sketches for people and getting paid. It's something I never imagined."

"Yes, many people go through life changes after recovering from a series illness," Joanna replied.

"Sure, but the thing is, every time I get into running or drawing a good sketch, that same peacefulness returns, and I don't think about much of anything. I'm totally focused on what I'm doing. Then, after I'm finished, I feel that same sense of completeness. It never was that way before. There's nothing better."

"I see," said Joanna.

Brandon sat tall. "I wanted to thank you again. I didn't understand all of that before and what incredible gifts they are."

The emotion had crept up Joanna's throat and she blinked her eyes. "You're welcome. I'm overjoyed that you made the most out of everything and found inner peace."

Brandon looked intently at Joanna. "Things are completely up to you. I needed to tell you-all this now because, no matter what you decide, I would hate to see you stop healing people. To stop giving other people those gifts." He slid his hand across the table towards Joanna. "I agree with Crystal in that whatever you decide, we'll be in it with you. I just worry if you deny everything to avoid Lucinda, you'll end up having to stop doing what you're capable of doing."

Joanna's hand met Brandon's, and she gave it a squeeze. "Now, I'm the one to thank you. That means so much to me." She let go of his hand then grasped her napkin. "Alright. Let's get back to these delicious pastries. Would you like a warmer in your coffee? It's no trouble. I'm going to get some for myself."

"Sure, that would be great, but you serve people all the time. I'll get it." Brandon was already standing with a hand extended towards her mug.

Try to Find Her

JOANNA BUTTONED HER SWEATER to get ready to leave but sat back down on the couch. The last couple of days seem to happen so quickly. Lucinda exposing her abilities. The support from Crystal and Brandon. The resistance from Sanders. It came as no surprise that he wasn't happy she was considering going through with the interview. Since then, the silence between them had been penetrating. Joanna retreated and spent a long day hiking the trails in the meadow, but there was no escaping what she needed to do. It was a way to bring healers together. After a deep breath, she stood up, walked across the room to the entryway, and opened the front door. The Lightmeadow Press offices were within walking distance.

As the office building came into sight, Joanna ignored any thoughts of turning back. She reached the steps and opened the door.

A young man sitting at a desk in a small waiting room immediately greeted her. "Hello, welcome to Lightmeadow Press. How can I help you?"

"Hi. I'm here to see Lucinda." Joanna scanned the room, sensing her own apprehension that someone she knew would pop in through one of the multiple doorways.

"Do you have an appointment?"

"No. Tell her Joanna is here. She'll know what it's about."

"Okay, you can have a seat, and I'll see if she's at her desk."

While Joanna chose a chair in the waiting room, she overheard the young man say, "Yes, I understand." Then he set the phone receiver back in the cradle.

Joanna looked at him, but he said nothing, and quickly shifted his attention to the array of papers in front of him.

A door opened to reveal a large room with rows of desks. Lucinda walked through the doorway and sat next to Joanna.

"Hello. I'm so surprised to see you," Lucinda whispered.

"Not as surprised as I am that I came." Joanna attempted a smile.

"And you are here for an interview?"

"Yes."

"As you probably noticed, the newsroom is a busy place. We can go into the conference room. It will be much more comfortable." Lucinda led Joanna through a door across the room. It revealed a traditional meeting room complete with a wooden table and leather chairs. Luckily, there was also a window to brighten up the space.

Lucinda did everything she could to make Joanna comfortable. She got them something to drink and situated her materials on the table. Before getting started, she even took off her suit jacket and flung it on the chair while casually chatting about the weather.

"No one will disturb us in here." Lucinda perched herself in a chair around the corner from Joanna. "Now, let's see. Do you mind if I record the interview? I won't share it with anyone and won't use any quotes unless you give me permission."

"Sure, you can record it," Joanna said.

"Great. So, let's start with some verification." Lucinda opened a folder and slid a photo of a middle-aged man onto the table. "Do you recognize him?"

Joanna picked up the photo and smiled. "Yes, I remember him. He came into the diner with his wife. I had guessed they were on vacation."

"Did you know he was ill?"

"Well, yes. It looked like he had a problem in his stomach, possibly cancer. The illness was located too high to be in his intestines."

Lucinda raised her eyebrows and wrote something on her notepad. "Did you intervene in anyway?"

"Yes, I went through the healing with him. He didn't know what it was, but he reacted to what I call the release. The release of energy, I guess."

"Did anyone else witness the, as you say, healing?"

"Yes, you were there and so I can't deny Crystal was there as well. She was serving the couple at the time."

"I noticed something happened." Lucinda grinned. "I'll also tell you; the man's name is Douglas Sharp. You were correct, he had stomach cancer. But shortly after he returned home, his nausea and fatigue subsided, so he went back to the doctor. He had a clear CT scan. The mass in his stomach had disappeared. The doctors have no explanation for how it healed."

Joanna vigorously nodded and handed the photograph back to Lucinda.

"I'll also tell you, he said he felt better than he had in years. He started gardening again. Said that he hadn't thought about it for a long time but realized he missed digging in the earth, making plants grow and the connection to the food he ate."

Joanna nodded again.

"Even more interesting, he said he tore his rotator cuff playing tennis during their vacation. The doctor gave him a picture to explain the injury, and he took it home." Lucinda pulled out a card with the anatomy of a shoulder and placed it on the table next to the picture. "For no reason at all, every morning after breakfast, he started spending ten or fifteen minutes closing his eyes and visualizing the tendon healing. He wasn't sure how much that had to do with it, but his shoulder got better in a matter of days."

Joanna shifted in her chair. "That's interesting. The part about going back to gardening sounds similar to what others have told me, but the meditation on an injury, I'm not sure, that seems like something more."

"Okay." Lucinda closed the folder. "So why don't you tell me what goes on when you do a healing. What it's like on your end and how you do it." She put her pen down, pulled her chair closer to the table, but leaned all the way back, giving Joanna more command of the space. "Take you time and be as detailed as you would like."

Joanna gave a detailed description of what happened when she detected illness and went through healing with someone. Then she talked about what she understood happened to the people afterwards. She finished with details about her relationship with her grandmother, who helped her to harness her talent. When she stopped talking, she stared at Lucinda and a silence lingered in the room.

Lucinda shook her head. "That's unbelievable, completely unbelievable."

"Yes, I suppose it is. But because I had the ability since I was young, it has always been with me. Part of my life."

"I see. And you said some things about your grandmother who guided you. Was she a healer too?"

"Oh, yes." Joanna replied.

"What about your mother?" Lucinda asked.

"If she was also a healer, she never let on."

"Interesting. But now, both of them are deceased, is that correct?"

"Yes."

"So that brings me to my next question. If you have this ability, how is it you can't make people live forever?"

"It doesn't work that way. It doesn't make people younger or anything." Joanna chuckled. "It's just sometimes, I'm able to heal them from a specific illness or, as a doctor would say, from a disease." She looked out the window for a moment. "In any case, no matter what we do, eventually the body loses the ability to protect and repair itself, then illness has the opportunity to become more pervasive. At that stage, as a healer, trying to control what is happening can be hurtful to them and myself."

"I don't understand. Can you explain that more?" Lucinda asked.

"Sure, give me a moment. It's hard to put into words." Joanna closed her eyes and took in a breath.

"I tried it once with my grandmother when she was very ill. The blackness had taken over most of her body, but I was young and didn't want her to go. So, I tried, and the process was the same except every stage was longer and more intense."

Joanna looked at Lucinda, who nodded, encouraging her to continue. "The love built up to a point where I never realized someone could experience that much love. At the same time, the energy built until it was bursting out of my body. Then when the release came, my head filled with an intense ringing and sharp pain." Joanna adjusted her posture. "When I got to the part where I momentarily black out, it felt like an instant yet lasted forever. My mind was there, but it was completely silent. There was no such thing as a thought. Everything was black and my body floated in a vast space." She thought about the memory. "It was floating but being pulled forward by the insides of my stomach."

"Then what?" Lucinda asked.

"I opened my eyes. And I heard my grandmother moaning in her bed. Trying to heal her had caused her pain." Joanna squinched her eyes shut before continuing. "But I also realized in that darkness, with just my consciousness, lies the answer. That all things are one and the same. That inner consciousness or what we might call the soul continues after death. And that dying is the way the soul transitions to a new state of being. Once things are in progress, when it's time, nothing is above that, and no one can stop it." She turned, put her hands on the table, palms up, and spread her fingers. "In that case the soul of the loved one benefits from our support during its transition."

Her hands glided together and clasped. "I'm certain that if I tried something like that again, the same thing would happen to reinforce the lesson."

"That's very moving." Lucinda sat quietly for a moment.

"Yes, as I mentioned, my grandmother guided me and she made me…" Joanna brought her hand over her forehead, a rush of memories thrusting into her mind. She was young, barely seven or eight. In the middle of a long winter, she had an episode of flu that turned into pneumonia. Late one evening, as the bitter wind howled outside, her mother and grandmother stood over her with ominous looks on their faces.

Joanna's grandma rung out a cloth with cool water and told her mother to go to bed. "Everything will be better in the morning. You'll see," Grandma had said.

"Joanna, are you okay?" asked Lucinda.

Joanna took a moment to shake off the persistent memories. "What? Yes, I'm fine." She rubbed her forehead. "Are we done yet?"

"Sure, we can be if you want to," Lucinda said.

"Yes, turn off the recorder."

Lucinda quickly leaned over and turned off the recorder. "It's off. Are you sure you're okay?"

"Yes, I just…" Joanna made deep eye contact with Lucinda. "This is off the record."

"Sure. Off the record." Lucinda dropped her pen and swept her hands over the table.

"What happened to the teenaged girl?"

"What girl?"

"The one visiting a sick relative at a hospital in Helinas."

"Oh." Lucinda opened another folder and pulled out a picture. "Do you mean her?"

Joanna grabbed the picture. It was from far away and a little blurry, but it was the girl that was in the diner with her parents. "Yes, that's her. You said you talked to her."

Lucinda sighed. "I talked to her, but I'm sorry she wasn't interested in talking to me and her mother was quite protective. It didn't go anywhere."

Joanna leaned across the table. "You have to try to find her. I just remembered my grandmother healed me when I was very young, and when she did, she passed the ability on to me. The way my grandmother described it was for the ability to continue on, it sometimes transfers between older women to younger women when they are healed." She slid the photo across the table towards Lucinda. "I may have done the same to her."

Lucinda's expression was stoic. "Well, I could try, but they were visiting in Helinas. I wasn't able to find out much about them, and don't know where they live."

"You have to try. Somehow, I was afraid this could happen. She has no one to guide her like I did and, worse yet, no one to *believe* her."

Lucinda picked up the photo and gave it a hard look. She put it back in the folder and reviewed her notes while clicking her tongue a few times. "Well, the mother said they were visiting a relative in hospice care. That person might be the owner of the house where they stayed. It will take some work and a little luck, but we'll give it try."

Exit for Lightmeadow

OVER THE REMAINING WEEK, Zoey worked on being able to stay grounded. She managed to keep the world from starting to disappear around every patient she encountered at the hospital. It became clear that whatever had changed wasn't going to go away on its own, so she did her best to forget about it all. As her father anticipated, her Aunt Erica, Uncle Rob and two of her cousins came to visit. She and her parents stayed at a hotel for one night and in the morning, they returned to the hospital.

Zoey walked in the front door with her parents. "Why don't we get Grandma some flowers before we go?" she asked before they passed the hospital gift shop.

"I think she would really like that," her mother said.

"You two go ahead. I'm going to see if I can catch the doctor and talk to Erica and Rob," her father turned towards the elevators.

The gift shop had attractive arrangements of flowers displayed behind a counter. Zoey and her mother discussed which Grandma would like best. They decided on a bright bouquet in a classic smooth white vase. At that point, they already had the attention of the sales associate, and her mother was telling him what they wanted while Zoey drifted over to the shelves of stuffed animals and small toys. She noticed a mini doll, just a little bigger than the size of her hand. It reminded her of Jessica, the little girl in the oncology playroom. The doll's body was soft with sewn in fingers and wore a cute plaid sundress. She picked up the doll. "Mom, can I get this little doll?"

"Well, sure, but why do you want it? It doesn't seem like something you would normally get," her mother asked.

Zoey shrugged. "I don't know. It's cute and fun. Maybe I'll give it to Grandma." She looked from the toy to her mother.

After her mother nodded, Zoey put the doll on the counter next to the flowers.

THE ELEVATOR DOORS OPENED on the floor with the hospice wing. Zoey walked alongside her mother and as they were at the junction between two hallways a child's voice called out, "There she is Mommy!"

Zoey swiftly turned in the direction of the voice. It was Jessica riding in a wheelchair pushed by the nurse, Kayla. There were balloons tied to the back of her chair and another woman was walking alongside while carrying a stuffed teddy bear.

Jessica pointed at Zoey. "That's her. It's the lady that was in the playroom."

Wide-eyed and stuck in place, Zoey stared at the scene.

"Do you know her?" her mother asked.

"Um yah, I guess. But I'm not sure how she would remember me," Zoey said.

Jessica's mother was the first to approach Zoey and her mother. "Hello, I'm Nancy Morgan, Jessica's mother." She extended her hand.

Her mother accepted Nancy's handshake and introduced herself and Zoey. Kayla quickly caught up to everyone with Jessica in the wheelchair.

"Look, I'm going home!" Jessica said.

"You're going home? That's great," Zoey replied.

"The doctor said my head is all better." Jessica pointed to the side of her head.

Nancy gazed at her daughter and said, "Yes, the doctors said she's in complete remission. They have no explanation how, but the tumor has disappeared."

"Well, that is wonderful news. I bet you're both very happy," Zoey's mother said.

"Uh-huh. Zoey was in the playroom with me when it happened," Jessica said.

"When what happened?"

"When my head got better. Something poked me and my head felt funny." The little girl put her head in one hand. "I was afraid then, but I'm not now. I'm all better."

Kayla was still hanging onto the handles of the wheelchair. She abruptly turned to Nancy and gave her a disapproving look.

Nancy tightened her lips. She met eyes with Kayla. "Would you give us a moment?"

Kayla let go of the handles and let her hands flop to her side. She returned to stand by the entryway doors of the oncology wing.

"My apologies. Many of the healthcare workers have their own point of view." Nancy squatted next to the wheelchair and put her hand on Jessica's arm. "We'll have to keep an eye on things, but the doctors were very thorough. No one knows exactly how everything happened or why we have been given this return to health, but we are beyond grateful."

Nancy's eyes were glossy with tears that tried to escape her lower lid. "And if my daughter says something happened in the playroom, then it happened. And if she says that's what made her better, then it's what made her better. There's no such thing as questioning a miracle." She rubbed Jessica's arm before standing up. "I'm so very glad I got the chance to meet you both."

Zoey had been clutching the doll so tightly that her fingers left imprints in the sundress and its soft body. She looked down at it and squished everything back in place before straightening the dress. She knelt in front of the wheelchair and handed the doll to Jessica. "Here, this is for you because I didn't get a chance to play dolls," she said.

Jessica sucked in a breath and grasped the little doll. She held it in the air, then tucked it in the crook of her arm. "It's so cute!"

"What do you tell your new friend?" Nancy prompted her daughter.

"Thank you, thank you very much," Jessica said, and she rocked the doll in a side-to-side motion.

"I would love to talk to you more, but we should be going now," Nancy said.

Overhearing this, Kayla returned to the wheelchair and started to push Jessica towards the elevators. Everyone exchanged quick well-wishes and, with one last wave from Jessica, they simply went on their way.

ZOEY TOLD GRANDMA ALL about her plans to take piano lessons, and Grandma told her more stories about how they played with the miniature piano. Her father returned from talking with the doctor and let them know Erica and Rob were in the waiting area. Zoey hugged her grandmother for a long time before leaving. She went to the waiting room where she talked with the other relatives until her parents returned. Once they finished their goodbyes, the stillness of the moment was striking, even though the exit from the hospice wing was drawing closer.

IN THE CAR, THE stillness continued to sit between the three of them as they got onto the road. Zoey tried to concentrate on her music, but the memories of seeing the blackness inside her grandmother's body, what happened with Jessica, and scenes from her nightmare rotated around and around in her mind as each mile passed. She gave up on the music and looked through her mother's *Woman's New Day* magazine. As she scanned the pages, a few things held her interest, but then a picture or title would take her back to the loop of memories.

Tossing the magazine aside, she looked out the car window just as they passed a sign announcing the exit for Lightmeadow was in ten miles. Finally, her mind came full circle and connected the tormenting memory loop with the details of her conversation with Lucinda and her experiences at the diner. She leaned forward closer to the front seat and asked her parents, "Can we stop at the diner? Isn't it time to get something to eat?"

"What diner?" her mother asked.

"The one in Lightmeadow, where we ate at on the way to visit Grandma," Zoey replied.

"Are you really *that* hungry? We were going to get dinner at Deville's and take it home. It will only be another hour or so."

"But I'm hungry and their food is good. Let's stop now. The diner is off the next exit." Zoey felt the car moving forward on the highway. "We have Deville's all the time."

Her father shifted in his seat and took his eyes off the road to look back at Zoey. "No. We're not stopping. We're driving straight through."

Cathleen placed her hand on Mitchell's shoulder and gave it a pat. She turned to Zoey in the backseat of the car. "It's been a long week and an exhausting day. If you wait, it will be good to get back home."

Zoey sat back in her seat. Another sign goes by on the side of the road, this time declaring the exit to Lightmeadow was in five miles. A lump gathered in her throat. In her desperation, she tried to push the topic. "Oh yah, remember that reporter? The one doing the piece on spontaneous healing. She's in Lightmeadow. Maybe she would like to hear about Jessica."

"That reporter? She was wrong to talk to you alone. And Jessica? Who's Jessica?" Her mother turned to her again, this time with a perplexed look, letting her mouth hang open.

Zoey couldn't contain the irritation brought on by her mother's expression. "Yes, Jessica. The little girl we met this morning who said she got instantly better, and the doctors didn't know why. The reporter might like to hear about that. It would be fun."

Her mother's expression remained unchanged. "You've got to be kidding."

Another sign passes, now the exit to Lightmeadow is three miles ahead. Zoey's irritation turned into a frantic feeling, like a cat with sharp claws trying to escape through a screen door. "Even Jessica said I was there when she got better. Maybe I had something to do with it and I could talk to the reporter lady."

Her mother furrowed her brow. "What are you saying? What's going on with you?"

"I just want… No, I need to talk to the reporter now." Zoey had raised her voice, carrying a hint of a yell.

"That's enough. As your father said, we aren't stopping." Her mother had matched her tone with an additional layer of parental authority. Then she robotically returned to looking out the front window.

Now Zoey had lost her mother's patience. The lump returned to her throat, and the emotions dug themselves deep in her stomach. She touched her fingers on the car window as they passed the exit for Lightmeadow.

What if They're Right?

ONCE ZOEY AND HER parents returned home, things quickly got back to their normal routine. The house was subdued as they all waited for news about Grandma's condition. Zoey found some refuge with friends at school, but the continual distraction of keeping the world intact around her hung on like a problem that had no resolution. In particular, her friend Sara seemed to have something wrong in her lungs, but Zoey kept herself from seeing it clearly. It seemed far better to ignore everything especially since the fallout from what happened in the oncology playroom and the dispute with her parents in the car.

In the middle of the week, Zoey found the house empty when she arrived home from school. She retrieved some granola from the cupboard and a glass of milk from the fridge before pulling out her Advanced Algebra book. Then she worked on her homework at the kitchen table. Even though she was into music, she liked the rhythm that the clear steps to solve a problem created. She was embarking on a second problem when she heard the garage door rumble.

"I'll be back down in a minute," her father said, followed by the sounds of his keys landing in the glass dish by the door.

Her mother walked into the kitchen and put her purse on the counter, along with some papers. "Zoey, you're here. Perfect. Your father and I had something we wanted to talk to you about."

Zoey moved her focus away from the algebra problem. "Oh, okay. I also have a question for you and Dad." She went back to her homework.

Her father came into the kitchen. "Hello Zoey. How was school today?"

"It was good. I have a question for you and mom."

"Sure, go ahead."

"A group of us are planning on going to the Balmar Cascades National Park for a camp out the weekend after next. Kind of a senior class weekend outing. I was wondering if I could use the car."

Mitchell exchanged a glance with Cathleen and slid his hands to his sides.

Zoey looked from her father to her mother. "I mean, I would take the Pontiac. I've always been a good driver and we are going to leave on Saturday morning and plan on being back on Sunday."

"It's not that. Honey, we have something to talk to you about too." Her mother sat in the chair next to Zoey and watched her father until he got seated in the chair across the table.

Zoey felt her fingers tighten around her mechanical pencil as her eyes studied their movements.

"We know dealing with your grandmother's illness has been difficult and after all the things that happened during the trip to Helinas, we've been concerned." Her mother gently put her hands together. "And since we've been back, you have been very withdrawn and haven't been eating the same foods you used to like so much."

"So, I've been eating better? Isn't that a good thing?"

"Well, yes, but it's not like you. It's different and we're worried about you."

Her father had been sitting tall while leaned back in the chair. He leaned closer and put his elbows on the table. "What your mother is trying to say is stress can get the best of anyone. But it's time for you to handle adult situations smoothly. So, we thought spending the rest of this school year, and possibly the summer, at a special retreat for young adults would be a good idea."

Zoey couldn't comprehend what she was hearing. So, she said a few off the wall things, and changed her eating habits, but it wasn't like she was out doing drugs or coming home drunk at night. "What are you talking about?"

Her mother got up and retrieved a paper from the counter. "See, here." She set a brochure on the table in front of Zoey. "This is the Javernick Center, and we were just there for a visit. It's beautiful and surrounded by woods with hiking trails." She opened the brochure. "You can go and take piano lessons, explore other arts, and study different subjects. They also have wonderful counselors to guide you in life skills and making a career plan."

"Counselors?" Zoey snatched the brochure and pointed at a picture. "That guy has a white coat on. He's probably a psychiatrist." She flung the paper, so all the folds of the brochure flipped open, and it landed flat on the table. In the middle of her inspection, she said, "What the hell is this place?"

"That's enough. This is a really great opportunity. I wish I could have done something like this when I was your age," her mother replied.

"Opportunity? You call leaving school and all my friends during my senior year to go to some teenage psych center an opportunity?" Zoey stared at her mother, then her father, who sat motionless. "Oh, I get it. You think I'm nuts; unbalanced and can't handle the real world just because I said a few things about seeing illness and wanted to talk to that reporter. Is that it?"

Her father slowly sat up in his chair again. "Look, if you can't see the benefit of going to Javernick, that's your own decision. But we both know that would be a mistake." His stare pierced Zoey's eyes. "You haven't even applied to any colleges, and you don't have a job."

"Well, no. But like Mom said, I plan on taking piano lessons and getting more serious about music."

"And how are you going to make a living doing that?" Her father's eyes darted towards the brochure. "If you don't go, you're telling me you're ready to be an adult. So, once you turn eighteen and graduate, get your own place. Find your own way."

"Oh, now Mitchell. Let's talk about this." Cathleen slid her hand in his direction.

Zoey got up from the table, grabbed her algebra book and scooped her papers on top. As soon as she headed for her bedroom, she choked in a sob that took her by surprise and picked-up her pace. In the threshold of her room, she slammed her bedroom door shut and leaned back against it. Another sob rose, and she slid to the floor, letting her book fall to her side. She couldn't remember ever feeling so terrible.

She hung her head in between her knees as she sobbed a few more times, followed by a few deep breaths. Suddenly she thought, *"What if they're right? What if it is the stress and emotions? What if when I think I'm seeing the insides of people who are sick, I'm actually hallucinating?"*

Zoey examined key events in her mind, starting with the diner, to the last time she was with her friend Sara. If she was hallucinating seeing the sickness and being able to do something about it, then Jessica getting better and the encounter with the reporter were just coincidences. *"Coincidences happen, right?"*

Maybe then her dream was a warning about how she was thinking. It was, after all, just a dream, a dreadful nightmare. It could have been telling her that the emotions were filling in the blanks, letting her see what she wanted to see so her hallucinations made sense. Hallucinations brought on by trying to escape that her grandmother was dying, and no one can make her better. That people die is a fact.

"Have I really lost touch with reality?" she asked herself.

Zoey released a gasp and crawled across the floor to her bed. She pulled herself up and fell into the soft comfort of the mattress. It took some effort, but she wormed her way under the covers, nestled her head into the pillows, and curled into a fetal position so she was facing away from the door. With the remnants of salty tears in the corner of her eyes, she dozed off until there was a soft knock on her bedroom door.

Zoey ignored the noise.

The door creaked part way open. "Zoey, honey. Can I come in?" asked her mother.

Again, Zoey didn't respond and remained curled up on her bed.

Her mother paused at the doorway. "Please, I'm going to come in. I just wanted to say a few things." She waited another moment before stepping into the room and quietly closing the door. Sitting on the edge of Zoey's bed, she continued, "I'm sorry you're so upset and can only imagine how difficult this must be for you. We don't say it enough in our household, but we love you and want the best for you. That's all." She leaned over and patted Zoey's shoulder. "Don't worry about what you father said, he was…"

Zoey turned part way to peer past her shoulder. "No, I'll go. I'll go to Javen-neck or whatever it's called."

"Are you sure?"

"I'm sure. I'll go." Zoey flopped over to lie on her back and stared at the ceiling.

"Alright. Let's talk about it if you change your mind or have doubts. In the meantime, you can go back to school so you can visit all your friends and we'll make the arrangements for you to start at the Javernick Center in the next couple of weeks."

Zoey thought about Sara. "No, I don't want to go back to school. If we're going to make the change, let's do it as soon as possible."

"Okay, we'll see what we can do." Her mother let out a deep breath. "Do you want to come down to the kitchen for some dinner? There's leftover chicken noodle soup."

Zoey's stomach growled so hard it almost hurt. "Okay." Puffy eyed and listless, she pulled the covers back and followed her mother to the kitchen.

Waves of Change

FROM THE BACKSEAT OF the Buick, Zoey watched as the car drove up the circular drive into the Javernick Center. The building was nestled in the woods and looked welcoming. It was reminiscent of an old southern plantation estate, complete with white paint and outside shutters around the windows.

Her father parked the car and the three of them walked inside. The receptionist's desk that looked like it also served as a security hub was in a large open entryway. On each side, two sets of stairs curved around to a second floor.

"Here we are," her mother said as her father talked to a gentleman at the receptionist's desk.

Soon, a young, well-dressed man in a white coat appeared. He greeted her parents; they had obviously met during their visit to the center. He spoke quietly to them, but Zoey could overhear the greetings followed by him saying, "From what you described, her situation seems acute, so she'll probably be placed at Level One. We'll have to see how the interview goes."

Her parents muttered words of agreement and seemed happy.

The man turned to Zoey and spoke in a comforting tone, "Hello Zoey. I'm Dr. Baskin and I'm here to assist with your initial assessment." He leaned forward in a deep nod. "After that, Connie will help you get settled. And of course, your parents will stay here during the intake process, and you'll see them again before they go." With an extended hand to guide

Zoey towards a hallway leading away from the entry-way area, he said, "Welcome to Javernick, we're glad you're here and hope you get the most out of your stay with us."

As they walked to the hallway Zoey could see be-yond the receptionist desk into a large dining hall with equally large windows that faced a landscaped area before the woods. Then the hallway was lined with offices and a few small rooms with chairs arranged in circles. Dr. Baskin's name was mounted on the wall next to one of the doors. He casually opened the door and invited her to have a seat. There was a small cof-fee table with a plant and a box of tissues surrounded by two chairs and a small loveseat. Zoey sat in one of the chairs and squeezed her arms in at her sides.

Dr. Baskin surprised her by sitting across from her on the couch instead of at the desk, where he had simply retrieved a clipboard.

"Okay," Dr. Baskin said before adjusting in his seat. "So, this is an initial assessment that helps us cur-tail a program that's right for you." He slid the clip-board onto the arm of the couch. "Before we get started, I want to be clear that anything you say in this room is confidential. I won't share any specifics with your parents. All I will tell them is what program we recommend and a general statement or two why. The best thing for you to do is to be as honest as you can."

"Yah, sure," Zoey crossed her arms.

"First, tell me why you agreed to come to Javer-nick."

Zoey answered all the questions with Dr. Baskin. She was mostly honest, telling him about what hap-pened at the hospital and in the children's oncology wing, but she stayed detached, keeping details and feelings to herself. She wasn't sure how this was going to go and wanted room to refine what she might tell them in the future. Despite having agreed to everything, she wondered why she stuck the business card from the journalist behind the lining of her suitcase.

Dr. Baskin clicked the pen into the holder on the clipboard and let it slide by his side. "That was great, Zoey. Thank you for answering all the questions so well."

Zoey held back a distinct urge to roll her eyes.

"Okay, I will take you to Connie's office, where you can work on your daily schedule."

CONNIE WAS A ROBUST woman with a warm voice that reminded Zoey of the type of person who had a large family. Outside of the core curriculum, they picked her other classes. Zoey included Music Appreciation along with piano lessons that they called, The Art of Piano. They didn't offer those courses at her high school, which was the upside to her schedule. On the downside, she was scheduled two sessions with a physiatrist and a group therapy session every week. Then she also had a session with a career coach every other week. Connie informed her that part of her schedule was just to start, and it would probably change after she was there awhile.

"*Three different psych sessions a week? That had better change. Otherwise, if I'm not a mental disaster now, I will be by the time I leave this place*," Zoey thought.

Zoey and Connie finished filling out all the paperwork. A few steps after they left the office, Connie told her they would meet her parents and Dr. Baskin in the lounge near the entrance.

In the lounge, her parents and Dr. Baskin were chatting about Javernick Center and how long the doctor had been there. They all stood up when Connie and Zoey entered the small room.

"Oh, honey. How are you doing?" her mother asked.

"I'm good," Zoey mumbled.

"Well, we are always just a phone call away. Dr. Baskin said you can have full privileges. Isn't that great?"

"Yah, sure." Zoey wrinkled her forehead.

They all sat down and went over details about visiting hours and having guests. Then her father got her suitcase and oversized duffle bag. The person at the receptionist table was one of the site supervisors at the center and when he came to get the suitcases, he simply said, "Hello everyone. My name is Sam and I'll take these upstairs."

She hugged both of her parents goodbye, and the energy of change swelled back and forth like waves on a vast ocean. Connie stepped in at an opportune time to address Zoey. "I'll show you to your room so you can get settled. Tomorrow, I'll guide you through your first day."

Zoey nodded and stepped closer to Connie. She looked at her parents and the emotions that had stuffed themselves into the bottom of her stomach stirred upwards. Her body felt limp, and her eye lids felt heavy. Following Connie's lead, she turned and walked out the door. She didn't dare look back to see her mother's attempt to follow her or strain to hear any of her father's words that would take them back to the crossroads where their minds meet.

Feeling Normal

ZOEY'S ROOMMATE WAS NAMED Amber, and she quickly got the idea Amber didn't talk much. The next day, Zoey was relieved when Connie held good to her word and guided her through her schedule. It took a couple of weeks until she was getting the hang of things.

Most of the residents at the Javernick Center came from families who had the means to send them there, but their personalities ranged every extreme Zoey could imagine. She also got the sense that some of them didn't care there was an entire world outside the confines of the center, or maybe they forgot that there was one. She missed her normal high school, and she missed her friends.

Many mornings Zoey woke up before her alarm and this morning was no different. At least she could get breakfast early and explore the hiking trails before her first class.

There were only a few people in the dining hall. Zoey got her breakfast and picked a table with a pleasant view of the forest. She took a sip of juice, and a stocky young woman who looked like she threw shot put on a regular basis clunked her tray on the table. The food on it giggled, and the silverware clinked.

"You don't mind if I sit here, do you?" asked the woman.

Zoey looked around at all the empty tables. "No, of course not."

The woman sat down. Then while holding her fork with her entire fist, she raised a hearty scoop of scrambled eggs into her mouth. She chewed with her eyes closed and swallowed with a subtle snap of her tongue. "Oh yah. That's what I'm talking about." She gestured with her fork. "I was starving." The woman took a few more bites before setting her fork back on the tray and wiping her hand on the side of her pants. With a hand extended across the table, she said, "Hi. I'm Mar."

Zoey reluctantly accepted the handshake. "Hi. I'm Zoey."

"Cool." Mar switched to munching her toast. "You know what the secret around here is, Zoey?"

"What secret?"

"You know, if you want more privileges and keep from going to the actual psych ward, you have to play their game. Just agree with everything and stay away from the meds."

Zoey wasn't sure how to respond. This was a completely new situation. "Well, I guess you're right."

"Damn straight I'm right. It's like, when I first got here, I told them I have a baby dragon who sits on my shoulder to protect me, and they went all ape shit." She dropped the remaining toast crust and started crumbling bacon with her mouth. "Put me on a cocktail of drugs that made me drool," she mumbled. "No one wants that shit."

"Yah, no. No one wants that," Zoey said.

"Damn straight." Mar took another bite of bacon, followed by a hearty swig of juice. "So, when they asked me about it again, I told them my dragon was gone. I must have made it up or something." She set the juice glass down. "Do you know what happened then?"

"No, what?" Zoey regretted her response the moment it went into her own ears.

Mar raised a bit out of her seat to match the volume of her voice. "Bam!" She sat back down. "Just like that, they weened me off most of the cocktail."

Zoey noticed Darren, one of the site supervisors, get up from the receptionist's desk. He slowly took a few steps in their direction with his thumbs tucked behind his belt.

"No more zombie land for me and there's no way I'm going back." Mar returned to eating the rest of her eggs.

Keeping quiet, Zoey did her best to remain casual and picked at her breakfast.

Mar finished her eggs and chugged the rest of the orange juice in her glass. She thumped the glass on the table and leaned back in her chair. Then she scooted the chair next to her and flopped one foot up on the seat. "Oh, that was good." She rubbed her stomach and let out a belch so loud it reverberated through the quiet room.

Darren approached the table with his thumbs still tucked in his belt, so when he stood, his waist thrust forward. "Is everything alright here, ladies?"

Mar had to look over her shoulder to get a full view of Darren. She stared just below his protruding waist. "Hey Darren. Yah, everything's alright. Just talking with Zoey." She shifted around and lifted her site up to his face. "Is everything alright with *you*?"

Darren rocked back on his heels. "Careful, Mar. You wouldn't want me to write a report. Those reports go into your psych file."

Mar turned away from him and mumbled something unintelligible.

"And get your feet off the furniture," he commanded.

Mar slid her foot off the chair, so it scraped against the seat and thumped on the floor.

Darren stared at her for a few hard seconds. His mouth moved as if he was going to say something more, but he turned and walked back to the receptionist's desk.

Aside from her eyes tracking each thing that was happening, Zoey couldn't move. It was like watching a scene in a movie that had a jolting twist.

Mar re-situated in her chair and smiled. "Oh, there you are." She turned to look just above her shoulder and made a petting motion in the air. "My baby." She changed her petting motion to longer strokes and made a few kisses with her lips. "What?" she turned to place her ear in the direction where she was making the petting motions.

After a few seconds, Mar turned to the side again. "No, I told you." This time, instead of petting, she pointed her finger to the air. "No more fires!" She jiggled her head from side to side. "How about you warm up mama's bacon?" Mar took a partial piece of bacon from her tray and held it in the air. "There, just a little." She turned the bacon from side-to-side. "That's right." She popped the bacon into her mouth and smiled.

Zoey's eyes were stretched open as wide as they possibly could be. She had to get out of the situation, but she could no longer think.

"Hey Zoey, want to go out to the benches?" asked a voice.

"Huh?" Broken from the trance, Zoey looked to where the voice was coming from. It was a young man she recognized from class. She didn't really know him, but he seemed nice.

With a smooth motion, he leaned to the side and put his hand on the back of Zoey's chair. "You don't mind Mar, do you?"

Mar allowed her attention to shift from, presumably her baby dragon, to the young man. "Oh, no. I don't mind. I have company of my own," Mar replied.

"Great." He turned to Zoey. "Are you ready?"

"Yah, sure. I have to dump my tray first." Zoey got up from the table. She grabbed her apple before tossing the partially finished breakfast. As soon as she placed her tray in the collection, she hurried to the door where her classmate was waiting.

They got out into the fresh air and walked to a cluster of benches arranged in a semi-circle between the hiking trails and athletics field. It was one of the few places anyone could sit and have a conversation without someone else in earshot.

"How about this one?" He headed for a bench that was getting early morning sun. "My name is Hunter, by the way."

"Hi Hunter," Zoey replied.

He sat on the bench, leaving plenty of room for Zoey. "So, you met Mar. She's Level Three."

"Level Three?"

"Yah, you know, how they put each patient into a level. Most of us are Level One or Two. There are a few Level Three patients, but they usually don't let them mix with everyone else."

"Oh." Zoey took a bite of her apple. She didn't understand it before, but she assumed she was Level One, since Dr. Baskin mentioned it to her parents and she had full privileges.

Hunter propped his foot on his knee. "The rumors are that Mar has super rich parents who are desperately trying to keep her out of the psych hospital." He leaned over and looked at Zoey. "And that the boys in her high school picked on her because of her brawn, so she set fire to their locker room."

Zoey coughed on a mouthful of half chewed apple and turned away from Hunter. She placed the back of her hand on her mouth before swallowing the bite. "Um, yah. I could see that."

"They have been letting her eat in the dining hall lately. Maybe the doctors think it will help her or something. I don't think it's going to work."

"Not from what I saw." Zoey took another bite from her apple.

"Yah, I get the feeling she won't be here much longer."

"I think you might be right."

"Anyway, what about Advanced Algebra? Are you into it?"

Zoey and Hunter stayed at the benches talking about life at Javernick as the rising sun altered the shadows. They critiqued their classes, laughed about group therapy sessions, and compared notes about the food. Despite her encounter with Mar that morning, Zoey felt normal for a moment. Then it was time to go to classes.

Zoey's first couple of classes moved by, and it was time for her session with Dr. Baskin. It turned out that he became her assigned psychiatrist. Just a few steps from his door, she heard voices coming from the office. It was unusual, so she paused and strained her ears to make sure he wasn't finishing with his previous appointment. It didn't take long before she figured out that he was with a colleague, and they were talking about her case. The realization glued her feet to the ground, and she kept listening.

"There's something that doesn't make sense. The idea that there is nothing to treat keeps creeping around in the back of my mind," Dr. Baskin said.

"You can't be serious. She's admitted she thinks she sees inside of people and can detect illness," his female colleague said.

Zoey assumed the colleague was Dr. Gould. She only met her once, but the two psychiatrists were also known to be close friends.

"Yes, but what about things like synesthesia? She's well-adjusted, intelligent, and creative. She's also interested in music. It could be a strange type of synesthesia that she can't identify properly," Dr. Baskin said.

"You're getting too close to your patient on this one. Let's go over it. Synesthetes have a clear bridge between two senses, like seeing colors when they hear music. Besides, she said this so-called ability recently appeared and she can repress it. That doesn't fit with synesthesia."

There was a long silence and Zoey held her breath so she wouldn't miss hearing the swishing sounds of movement. The last thing she wanted was to get caught eavesdropping on their conversation.

Finally, she heard Dr. Baskin continue, "Sometimes I don't know how we're supposed to help our patients if we don't believe them in the first place."

"You always have been an idealist," Dr. Gould chuckled and paused. "Although I had a case similar to this one about a year ago. It was very similar." She sighed. "What was her name? Something in nature. Weeds. No, Woods." She snapped her fingers. "That's it, Cassandra Woods. I'll pull the file and you can take a look at it."

"That would be helpful, thanks," Dr. Baskin said.

Zoey took a few silent steps backwards, then re-approached the office to mimic that she had just arrived. "Oh." She stopped one step past the doorway. "I'm sorry to interrupt. I can wait outside."

"No, no. Dr. Gould and I were just finishing. Have a seat."

Zoey got settled in the same chair she sat in during her intake interview. It had become her normal chair. While the two psychiatrists finished their conversation, she used the time to scribble the name of Dr. Gould's patient on a page in her notebook and put it with her books on the floor next to her chair.

As her session got started, she relaxed and took part for a change. Dr. Baskin let her guide the conversation, so she made the most out of it by talking about her relationship with her overprotective mother, how her father was reacting to Grandma being in hospice care and worries about her independent future. It was a surprise to her, but some of it was helpful.

Zoey felt normal for the second time that day and sprinted up to her room before going to the dining hall for lunch. When she reached the room, she was glad it was empty. She quietly closed the door. After pulling the suitcase out from under the bed, she searched under the lining in the bottom. Her fingers grasped Lucinda's small business card, and she brought it to eye level.

Zoey flipped the card over and wrote down Cassandra Woods, the name of Dr. Gould's patient. Then she wrote Jessica and stopped. *"What was her mother's name and their last name?"* she asked herself. She closed her eyes and tried to focus. *"Nancy… Nancy… How am I going to remember?"* She let her mind visualize the scene in the hospital hallway when Jessica's mother introduced herself and shook hands with her mother. *"Nancy Morgan. That's it!"*

She wrote the name on the back of the card. Once finished with her task, she returned the business card to its hiding place and put away the suitcase. She tore the page out of her notebook with Cassandra's name on it and shredded it into tiny pieces. She gathered up her books for afternoon classes and slowly opened the door.

On her way back to the dining hall, Zoey stopped in the bathroom. In one of the many stalls, she tossed the tiny pieces of paper into the toilet bowl. Then she sat down, relieved her bladder, and flushed the toilet. In the stream of the industrial flush, the pieces of paper swirled and disappeared without a remote chance to protest. She walked out of the stall, washed her hands, and used the mirror to straighten her shirt.

Part way down the stairs, Zoey wondered if Mar would be in the dining hall having lunch with everyone. She slowed her steps and calculated that there would be many people having lunch by now and she would pick a table that was mostly full. Possibly a table closer to the receptionist's desk where the site supervisor sat. There would be plenty of time to survey the situation while she was filling her tray. As it turned out, in ways her father would have never predicted, Zoey was learning to enter the adult world in a big way.

Witchy Waitress

JOANNA RETURNED TO THE diner for another shift. She normally would work as a closer, but Gus was short on day servers, so she agreed to work the morning. She used her keys to let herself inside. The diner was already filled with the smells of fresh coffee brewing and breakfast sausage sizzling.

Crystal rushed over to Joanna with a newspaper in her hand. "Did you see it? Lucinda published the article."

"Already? She said it was coming, but I didn't think it would be this soon." Joanna grabbed the paper and opened the fold. "The front page?" She read the simple title, "Hometown Healer."

"It's a really good picture of you."

"I let Lucinda talk me into taking some shots in the meadow." Joanna put her hand on her forehead. "I didn't think it would be on the front page."

"Well, yah. This is big news around here." Crystal adjusted her apron and turned to the side. "The article is actually pretty good." With a slight shrug, she left to finish prepping her tables.

Joanna sat in the closest chair. Without a care that the diner was about to open, she read the article. She was so focused that she jumped when Gus's voice broke her concentration.

"So, you're a bit of a celebrity now," Gus said.

"I guess so." Joanna looked at him with a blank stare.

"Well, good for you. I think some folks around here kind of knew, especially after Brandon got better."

"Oh."

Gus wrapped his knuckles on the table a couple of times. "Now, you take care. Let me know if you need anything. I've always thought of you and Crystal as my sisters."

"Sure, thank you." Joanna eyes scanned Gus's large outline guarding over her and returned to stare at the article. She felt stagnate thinking take over, and the words blurred together. It took a couple of shakes of her head to get herself to refocus and finish reading each word.

Gus had already opened the doors to the diner, and a few regulars filled the seats. Many of them gravitated to the counter, so Joanna had time to get ready before the breakfast rush. She was thankful for the work that kept her mind off everything. The peak of the rush came and went, and the morning continued the same as most any other day.

Joanna was pre-bussing a table when Ratlin came in the entrance. He gave her a wave and slid into a booth in Crystal's section. From the looks of his jacket, it was raining outside. She looked out the front windows, and the bright sunrise had turned into a gray overcast day, spitting showers onto the ground.

After dumping off her dishes, she stopped by Ratlin's table. "How are you this morning?"

"Hi Joanna. I'm fine, just fine." He leaned back in the booth and brought out his boyish smile. "So how did it go with Gus? Is he interested in the book for the giftshop?"

"Oh, yes." Joanna rubbed her hands down her apron. "Let me see if he's available so you two can work out the details."

"Great."

"I'm sure Crystal will be by to take your order shortly."

Joanna headed to the kitchen and looked in Crystal's direction. Crystal's face brightened when she spied Ratlin in her section and she looked at Joanna so they could share a smile, even if it was for a brief second.

Joanna wove through a few people in the kitchen. Some of them were already prepping for lunch. Reaching Gus, she relayed the message about Ratlin, and he grunted.

"Tell him I'll be out in a few minutes." Gus pulled an order ticket down from the rack. "When I get a few more orders done, Donnie can handle the window."

Joanna looked at Donnie, the second cook, and he pinged his metal spatula against the griddle, flipped it in the air and snagged it on its way down, all with a smile.

Joanna chuckled and returned to the dining area. She gave Ratlin a quick thumbs up on her way to rotate through her tables with breakfast in progress. Eventually, her incoming customers slowed to a sporadic pace.

Joanna couldn't miss Crystal's beaming smile. In their usual synchronization, the two women looked at each other and met where the booths divided their sections.

"Ratlin just left," Crystal said.

"Uh-huh." Joanna joined Crystal in watching him get into his truck.

"Yah, so Gus is putting his book in the giftshop. He'll be back."

"I guess so." Joanna inspected Crystal's profile. "You really like him. Don't you?"

"I don't know. I guess so." Crystal fell silent in brief thought. "He seems kind, considerate, and very deep. All those things." Her hand raised and twisted one of her curls around her finger. "But, yet it's like he's lived a whole other life. He's certainly not like the men around here."

"That's for sure," Joanna said as Ratlin's truck pulled out onto soppy roads.

Joanna was about to return to business when Crystal turned her head to the direction of the entrance to the parking lot. Joanna followed her line of vision, and a van was pulling in, which was a regular occurrence. But the van was quickly followed by two more cars and then another van.

"It must be a travel group," Crystal said. She turned to the pickup window and called out, "Gus, we have a travel group coming in."

"Got it." Gus's voice boomed in the kitchen. "Donnie, start prepping."

"Wait, a minute." Joanna watched the people pile out of the vehicles and retrieve large items from the trunks of the cars. "What are they doing?"

"I don't know. They look like signs," Crystal replied.

"You're right. But I can't read them from here." Joanna squinted her eyes, trying to focus through the cloudy drizzle. The group, armed with rain slickers, gathered and one man put a bullhorn to his mouth. They could hear the vibrations of his voice, but it was impossible to make out a word he was saying. With a wave of his arm, he directed the small crowd toward the diner. The crowd clapped and a few of them cheered. As they drew closer, Joanna read the first visible sign out loud, "The devil lives in witchcraft."

"Oh my," Crystal said. "What does that one say?" She moved her finger to follow another sign one of the van riders held while they walked closer. This time she read out loud, "Until today, witchcraft was an invisible crime."

"What in the world?" Joanna leaned closer to the window. Another sign came into focus. She gasped and stumbled backwards. Falling back, she grabbed the edge of a table and managed to clench her other hand onto a chair back, so she didn't end up sitting on the floor. She mumbled what the sign said, "The waitress is a witch."

"It's okay." Crystal came behind Joanna and pulled her upwards so she would stand up straight. "Really, it will be okay." She left one hand lanced under Joanna's arm.

Joanna could see out the window again, and what she saw was almost more than she could endure. A middle-aged woman holding hands with a young girl, probably her daughter, was falling in with the pack of people. The girl held a sign that said, "Witchy Waitress," and it looked like there was a Halloween caricature of a witch drawn in the corner.

With a gasp, Joanna covered her mouth as her face filled with heat. Crystal used her arm to leverage Joanna towards the break room. "Okay, that's enough." She pulled Joanna to encourage her to start taking steps. "Let's get you away from the window." Still assisting Joanna, she yelled towards the kitchen, "Gus, get out here."

Clatter came from the kitchen, followed by Gus rushing into the dining area. He scanned the room, and as soon as his eyes set sight on Crystal guiding Joanna to the back of the diner, it only took him a couple of steps to get close to the women.

"Check the parking lot." Crystal said in a clenched whisper.

Gus leaned over and looked out the front windows. His eyes met the area near the door where the group had gathered. "What the hell?" He wasted no time. "Ronnie, get on the phone to Lightmeadow Police Department and ask for Officer Hanley. Tell him we have protestors trespassing on the diner's property."

Gus grumbled and said, "I'm going out there."

Finally, in the confines of the break room, Joanna quietly got comfortable in a chair.

"Sit a minute, take a deep breath." Crystal looked back at the door. "I'm going to see how things are going." She smiled as if she relished the excitement and snuck out a half-opened door.

Joanna wasn't sure what was worse, sitting alone with her thoughts or being a target for such ridicule. She closed her eyes and, as Crystal suggested, took in a deep breath. The exhale came easy as she drew her lips closer together and felt the breeze move from the back of her throat to the outside of her body. She kept her eyes closed and repeated the process two more times. Then she remembered telling Crystal about how, if more people knew about her abilities, she might be able to bring healers together and her conversation with Brandon. Once she opened her eyes, she stood up and left the confines of the break room.

As she walked to the dining area, Joanna looked down to straighten her apron and almost bumped into Crystal. The two steadied themselves and laughed.

"Tonight, I can go home, relax with a glass of wine, and take a hot bath, but for now, I need to go on with my day," Joanna said.

"Good for you." Crystal nodded and smiled.

Gus grabbed their attention when he came in from confronting the protestors. He met up with the two women near the kitchen entrance.

"So, what happened?" Crystal asked.

"Oh, they're some church group or something from Helinas. They gave me a little pushback, but they moved off the property." Gus looked out the window with a grin. "Let's see how long they like it on the sidewalk getting sprayed by passing traffic." He tromped to the kitchen.

Joanna returned to her tables. On the way around her station, she noticed the squad car pull in and slowly circle the lot. It rolled to a slow stop alongside the protestors before pulling back out onto the street. Right where she stood, she closed her eyes and took a deep breath through her nose, then reminded herself to go on with her day. A secondary wave of breakfast customers had been coming in and she went back to business, letting the familiar work take her mind off everything else.

Two couples got comfortable in a booth in Joanna's section. She gathered their drinks and returned to take their order. Of course, the man and woman by the windows were watching the group on the sidewalk. The woman turned to Joanna. "What is that all about?" She looked at her companions at the table. "A little extreme, if you ask me." They laughed and turned their attention to Joanna.

"Oh." Joanna wasn't sure how to respond. She felt a tinge of panic and wondered if they could read the signs, or worse yet, had seen her picture and the article. "Oh, it's nothing. It's just a church group from Helinas." With the eyes of everyone at the table still upon her, she shifted to the side. "Can I get you anything else?"

The group at the table was settled with their orders, so Joanna gladly continued on her way. At the pickup window, she stopped to take another deep breath and repeated her new mantra to herself. "*Wine and hot bath tonight, but for now I need to go on with my day.*"

Joanna continued her shift and avoided lengthy conversations about the activity outside. Her side work that day included one of her least favorite tasks, cleaning and filling the ketchup bottles. It was something about the vinegar smell that made her face grimace.

Crystal swerved over and gave Joanna a smile. "Only one more hour and you'll be finished here for the day." She leaned back as she took a step away. "You're going to make it."

On her way back to her section, Crystal stopped and looked out the window. "It looks like they're leaving." With a bend to lower her gaze and a step closer to the window, she said, "Oh, yes, they are on their way out." She made a little wave towards the window. "Bye, bye nutty church group." With a turn of her head, she looked at Joanna and let a smile grow that made small creases behind her eyes.

Joanna nodded with a grin and returned her focus to the disdaining side work. At that moment, she was sure that Crystal was relishing the excitement. A few of Joanna's existing tables still needed attention, but soon as she was done with her shift, she headed for the door.

Gus's voice traveled from the pickup window. "Joanna, hold on. Let Ronnie walk you to your car."

Joanna turned to meet Gus's stare with the most intense look she could muster, but Gus's eyes never laid off. Certain Ronnie was about to pop out of the kitchen at any second anyway, she called out, "Fine Ronnie, let's go."

In her car, Joanna gave Ronnie a wave and watched him walk back to the diner. As soon as he was out of sight, she let her head fall on the steering wheel. After the meditative pause, she lifted her head, turned the key to the ignition, and pulled out of the parking lot.

Taillights Disappear

THE DRIVE FROM THE diner to Joanna's home was short. As she neared the driveway, her irritation rose, and heat flooded her face again. The protestors hadn't returned to Helinas. They were gathered on the sidewalk in front of her house. The rhythmic beats of their chanting carried through the drizzle outside and through the closed car windows.

It was out of the ordinary, but Sanders had parked his car out on the street. Joanna let out a breath filled with relief and pulled into the drive. The protestors raised the level of their chants at her passing car. She parked close to the backdoor to avoid getting in direct eyesight of the persistent group.

The car door creaked as it opened, and she got out of the car. Now she could hear their words, *The devil lives in witchcraft*. They paused. *The waitress is a witch*.

Joanna unwillingly dashed for the backdoor and her hands were shaking as she brought the key to the lock. Before she turned the key, Sanders flung the door open from the inside.

"Come on, get in here," he said.

Joanna brushed by him, embracing the warmth inside the house. She wanted to fall into Sander's arms and feel his firm embrace. But as she watched him thump the door shut and firmly twist the bolt lock, that idea faded into a forgotten fantasy.

Joanna kept her eyes on Sanders as he walked by her without a word. She followed him through the backdoor into the kitchen. As usual, she went to the front entryway closet to put away her coat and take off her shoes. There, sitting by the front door, were two large suitcases. "What is this all about?" She glanced around the corner and continued back to the kitchen, where Sanders was leaning against the island counter. "What are the suitcases all about? Do you think we should leave?"

Sanders looked at the ground. While returning his eye contact with Joanna, he said, "I'm leaving." He rubbed his hand across his mouth. "They offered me the promotion in Helinas, I think they already had it mind when they hired me. I accepted and most of my things are packed. I'm ready to go."

"Are you serious?" Joanna threw her stare across the room. "You're leaving right now? With all this going on?"

"That's right, Joanna." He gestured towards the front of the house with his hand. "I warned you that the article would be disruptive. This is too much. Even a news crew was out there earlier." He let his hand fall to his side and shifted to his soft voice. "I would love for you to come with me and start a new life in Helinas."

With nothing more to say about moving to the city, Joanna maintained her stare and took a step further into the kitchen. She noticed his stylish hair and button shirt were unusually disheveled.

Sanders continued on his own. "But either way, I will not let this ruin my chances at a successful career. What am I supposed to say to them? Oh, sorry, I can't start right now." He spun to the side, talking to an imaginary person, and raised his voice. "You see, my partner is being stalked by a bunch of fanatics because she thinks she can heal people."

The sound of Joanna's heartbeat raised into her ears. "I see." She stood straight and slightly raised her chin a bit. "If that's how you feel about it, then you should go."

"Joanna, I'm sorry."

Joanna put up her hand and took a step away. "Just go. Don't make this worse than it already is." She walked into the living room and sat on the couch. She watched Sanders pick up the suitcases and open the door.

"Again, I'm sorry," he said.

Joanna sat back in the couch cushions and looked across the room until the door shut tight. As soon as his footsteps outside went silent, she got up and peeked out the window. Of course, the protestors raised their volume as he walked down the drive. Unaltered by their attention, he put the suitcases in the trunk, got into the driver's seat, and drove away. Her eyes stayed on the car taillights until they disappeared in the mist.

Furious at his words and that he would leave after all the years she supported him, she turned and kicked the pincushion footstool. The small stool caught air and flew into the side table. The table wobbled, and the glass vase sitting on top tumbled to the floor, where it splintered into pieces.

Joanna stared at the vase, wondering how to fix something with broken pieces that will never go back together the way they were before, until the doorbell rang.

The sound of the bell made her suck in her breath and place her hand on her chest. Adrenaline made its entrance, and her pulse quickened. She looked around the room and considered finding a spot where she could remain unseen while she ignored the unknown visitor. Instead, she took a deep breath and her mantra returned. "*Wine and hot bath tonight, but for now I need to go on with my day,*" she thought.

Creeping up to the door, she pulled the curtain back to see who was standing on her porch. It was Lucinda, who took a moment to yell something at the protestors.

Joanna swung the door open. "Lucinda, what are you doing?"

"I couldn't help myself." She glanced back at the group. "I'm so sorry about all this mess. Can I come in a minute?"

"Yes, of course. Come in. Let me hang up your coat." Joanna took Lucinda's damp coat and hung it across two hooks.

"I hope I'm not disturbing you." Lucinda looked around. "Like I said, I'm sorry about the protest group and all. I had no idea."

"Thanks, but you couldn't have known." Joanna scrupulously scanned Lucinda's face. "I was just about to open a bottle of wine. Would you like to have a glass?" Joanna didn't wait for an answer before heading straight to the wine rack in the kitchen. She was scanning the bottles and selected her favorite chardonnay before Lucinda made it to the kitchen.

"Have a seat." Joanna placed the bottle on the counter and produced two wine glasses from a cupboard. "Well, the front page. I was surprised."

"I thought you knew. Another reason to apologize. I should have made that clear." Lucinda sat halfway into a chair and inspected the room. Her eyes scanned the clean rectangle on the wall, the remnants of an imprint where a picture was recently removed, and the dust balls scattered around the floor.

Joanna brought the two glasses over to the table and melted into a chair. "You don't have to apologize for your success." She put her feet, comfortable in thick white slouch socks, on the chair next to her. With her eyes closed, she took a sip of her wine. "Well, this has been quite the day."

"That's for sure." Lucinda brought the wineglass to her nose, then took a slow sip. "Oh, that's good." She set down the glass. "I suppose you're right. I don't have to apologize for my success, but I'm glad I stopped by."

"Thanks, but that's just the wine talking." Joanna laughed.

"No, really!" Lucinda swiped her hand across the table and laughed. She leaned back in her chair. "I also have an update on locating the teenage girl."

"Really? How wonderful. I'm so worried about her."

"We've found the parents. As it turns out, the father is related to the owner of the house where they stayed." She took a sip of wine. "The family lives in a small town called Greybel, but…"

"But what?"

"It's kind of odd. We staked them out a little, and it's definitely the same couple, but it seems the daughter isn't living at home right now."

"Where is she?"

"I don't know." Lucinda did a rapid shrug. "If we have the right individual, she isn't eighteen yet, so she must be with a relative, or somewhere with her parent's permission."

"Oh." Joanna leaned back in her chair and stared at the table.

"Zach, our investigator is still looking for her." Lucinda picked up her glass, swirled the wine and looked at it through the light. "Hopefully, he'll turn something up."

Joanna shifted closer to the table. "Please keep searching."

Lucinda nodded and inspected around the kitchen again. "So, where's Sanders? I would expect he wouldn't leave you long with the protestors outside."

Joanna let the rest of her wine slide down her throat. "He left." She retrieved the bottle from the counter. "More?"

"Sure, thanks." Lucinda slid her glass across the table. "What do you mean, left?"

Joanna got situated in her chair again. "Just what I mean, left." She waved her hand across the room.

"You mean he's not coming back? He left you in the middle of all this?"

"Pretty much, yes."

"Of all the terrible things." Lucinda pursed her lips. "What a lowly little self-centered coward. To leave you when things get a little challenging." She took a hearty sip of wine. "Well, better you found it out now rather than later."

"So true." Joanna sighed. "Can't say I didn't see it coming. He's wanted to move to Helinas for months."

"He left for Helinas?"

Joanna nodded.

"And, let me guess, you were just supposed to drop everything and leave the house that has been in your family for generations?" Lucinda leaned back in her chair. "Of all the nerve."

Joanna looked around the kitchen. "Even so, I didn't expect it would happen the second things shifted, and I was the one who needed something."

A still silence filled the kitchen until Lucinda stood up so quickly her chair slid back. With a swift motion, she grabbed the bottle of wine. "Come on. Let's go sit in the living room and be comfortable." She took a step away from the table. "Let those protestors get glimpses of us doing what we would normally be doing."

Joanna grinned and held up her glass. "Yes, let's go on with our day."

He's a Little Grubby

A BEAM OF SUNLIGHT creeping in between the curtains hit Joanna's eyes. She rolled over in bed and snuggled back in, but something urged her to keep moving. *"What time is it?"* she wondered. The clock next to the bed read eight o'clock, and she sprang to a sitting position. With her mind hazy from wine and late-night conversation, she remembered Lucinda's visit lasted until after the protestors left. Worried the group might have returned, she strained her ears but couldn't even get a hint of their rhythmic chanting. She pivoted her head in each direction, but still there was nothing but silence.

Joanna tied her robe on the way down the stairs. Her feet pattered each step and crossed the cold tile floor to the front window. Not a person in sight. She let out a chuckle and scanned up and down the street. Turning from the door, she looked around and digested that Sanders was also gone. Nowhere in sight. At that point, she figured, the only thing to do was to make coffee, enjoy a cup, and let her memory process the events. But once her mug was empty, she had to get ready for work.

BACK IN HER NORMAL closing shift, the diner was picking up at its usual pace. Joanna moved along with little effort, taking care of her tables. Some customers asked her about the article, but most of them expressed a wide-eyed curiosity about it all. She played it safe and answered their questions by rephrasing parts of the article.

Joanna had just taken checks to her tables when Travis walked in with another person. Unlike Travis, he was tall, skinny and had thick blonde hair. With his companion in tow, Travis seemed even more domineering. They got into a booth in her section. She took a deep breath before approaching the table.

"Hello Travis. Can I get you guys something to drink?" she asked.

"Yah, and we'll order now." He put down the menu and looked at Joanna. "This is my distant cousin, Ned. He's here from out of town."

Travis's eye contact sent an unsettled feeling that traveled into her gut. She looked to the other side of the booth. "Hi Ned. Nice to meet you."

Ned looked at her and used his hand to raise his ball cap a bit.

Ned's wisp of eye contact didn't feel so great either. Joanna moved the process forward. "Okay, what can I get for you?" She took their order and went on her way.

Another couple had chosen the booth next to Travis and Ned. Joanna stopped by the new booth, and the couple was holding hands and laughing. They quickly acknowledged her and slid back from one another.

Joanna introduced herself and proceeded to drink orders. She looked at the woman and the familiar sensation of the world starting to disappear crept up on her. The visual of a black oval on the side of the woman's breast was clear. She probably had breast cancer.

"Are you okay?" the man at the table asked.

The question pulled Joanna out of the slight trance, and she readjusted. "Sorry, I'm fine. I got distracted." She put her hand on the side of her head and pulled it away with a wave. "I'll get your drink order." With a weight on her chest, she walked away from the couple. After everything that happened the last couple of days, there was no way she could risk calling more attention to herself and help the woman while she was at the diner.

The drinks became an extension of the tray as Joanna glided back to the tables. She delivered them to both booths. The food orders for Travis's table were up, so she retrieved the dinners and returned to the table. After serving the plates, Joanna asked, "Is there anything else I can get you?" With caution, she glanced at each side of the table.

"So, is it true you can heal people? People that are sick?" Travis asked without looking up from his plate.

"Um yes, sometimes." Joanna took a micro step back. "You got to see the article?"

"Yah, mostly." Travis dug into his fries and Ned had already taken three bites out of his burger. They continued eating without a word.

"Okay, so I'll be back to check on you." Joanna stepped away and stopped at the other booth to take the couple's dinner order. When Joanna put in the ticket, Crystal was at the serving window.

Crystal arranged a few plates in the window, then looked at Joanna. "How are you doing?"

"I'm okay, given everything." Joanna glanced across the room. "One woman in my section looks like she has early breast cancer, but there's nothing we can do right now."

Crystal looked at Joanna for a moment before her face brightened. "I know. Why don't you give her a copy of the paper?"

"What do you mean?"

"Give them a copy of the newspaper with the article. At least they'll get the information." She picked-up the strategically arranged plates. "It's a start."

"I guess you're right. There are some papers behind the counter in the giftshop." Joanna smiled then looked over at her other booth. "Now, if you could get Travis out of my section, he's here with that other guy and acting kind of strange tonight."

"If you ask me, Travis always acts strange. And who is the other guy? He looks a little grubby." Crystal rolled her eyes.

"That's Travis's cousin of some type. Said his name was Ned."

"Well, it's your turn. Travis was in my section last time." Crystal smirked and took the plates out to her tables.

Joanna circulated through her other tables before returning to her back-to-back booths. She took the food out to the couple and checked-in on Travis and Ned. Finally, she got their checks ready. The extra copies of the newspaper were easy to find, and she slid one off the top of the tidy stack. She dropped off the check for Travis and Ned on her way to the other booth. After pre-clearing the couple's table, she set down the paper and check. "Here's a newspaper, complements of the diner and your check is ready."

"Thank you. A local newspaper, how interesting." The man stared at the folded paper for a second before pulling a credit card out of his wallet. "Here you are." He handed the check back to her with the card.

Joanna took their payment and cashed them out. Meanwhile, she spied Travis and Ned leaving cash on the table then wandering towards the exit. When the door closed behind them, she waited to feel lighter, but the sense of relief never came. She scanned the room and continued circulating through her tables.

As it always does, closing time arrived. Joanna and Crystal slowed their pace to work on prepping the tables for the next day. While they worked, Joanna caught up with Crystal about Sanders leaving and Lucinda staying until the protestors left.

"Oh, Joanna. I had no idea all that happened last night." Crystal finished wiping a table with neatly stocked condiments in the center. "You are strength upon strength." She gave Joanna a curtsey.

"Thank you." Joanna curtseyed back. "But I'm still waiting for a hot bath. And that may be when I have a nervous breakdown." She finished the table she was working on and moved to the next.

A working silence lingered until Crystal blurted out, "What is that?"

"What?" asked Joanna.

Crystal raised her voice. "Is that Travis peeping through the window?"

Joanna's fingers release her dishtowel, so it fell onto the table. She followed Crystal's line of vision over to the window. In her edgy state, she jumped back with a partial squeal. It was Travis leaning over the bushes trying to get a look inside the diner. The landscaping lights illuminated his face, making him look like a crazy stalker. She pushed a chair to the side, creating a clear path to get next to Crystal and said, "What in the world is he doing?"

Clatter carried from the kitchen and Gus followed into the dining area. "What's going on?" He looked back and forth at the two women.

Crystal leaned in Gus's direction and waved her hand towards where they saw Travis. "Travis was peeping in through the window."

Joanna returned Gus's traveling eye contact and nodded.

"That big ass. I'm going to make sure he's gone." Gus stomped his way out the door.

Joanna looked at Crystal who grinned and returned to wiping another table. Her cloth moved in circular motions as she sang in a repeated melody. *"They call him cree-pee. Creepy the peep-pee."* After a second round, she looked up and laughed.

"You're enjoying all this excitement. Aren't you?" Joanna asked.

"Well, I wouldn't quite put it that way." Crystal grinned. "I just like helping my friend and experiencing something that's out of the Lightmeadow normal."

"Uh-huh." Joanna picked up her dishtowel and flung it at Crystal. It hit her side and fell to the ground.

Crystal looked at Joanna with an exaggerated pout and the two women burst out in laughter. Then the sound of the front door flinging open and Gus's heavy footsteps crossing the threshold subdued their bantering.

"Well, I didn't see anyone out there." Gus rotated a wooden baseball bat in his hand, so it flopped into his freehand with a smack. "I don't like that kid so much." He glared out the windows as he walked.

Joanna took a few steps. "Gus…"

"What?" Gus stopped at the entrance to the kitchen.

"Say, where did you get that baseball bat?" Joanna asked.

"I grabbed it out of my truck." Gus stroked the barrel of the bat with his eyes and his hand. "I put it in the back when we had problems with the vandals. It makes me feel safe, somehow." He looked at Joanna. "It also reminds me of when I was a kid so, it keeps me calm." Then he disappeared into the kitchen.

Joanna turned her attention to Crystal and did a full-fledged shrug.

Gus came back into the dining area. "And I want you two to let me know when you're leaving so I can make sure you get to your cars safely. Okay?"

"Absolutely," Crystal replied.

Gus returned to the kitchen while Joanna and Crystal went back to finishing their work for the night. The dining room was ready for the next day when Joanna called out, "Gus, we're ready to go now." She removed her apron and tucked it into her duffle bag.

Crystal trotted out of the break room. "Yah, Gus, we're ready."

Gus came out of the kitchen with his baseball bat in hand. "Alright. Let's go." He ushered the two women out the side door. "If anybody's out there, let's make sure they don't come back." He chuckled.

They walked out onto the loading dock and the women continued down the stairs, leaving Gus to his high vantage point. He stood smacking his baseball bat into his palm and feet wide apart.

Joanna wasn't sure what to make of Gus's performance. In her car, she had to linger a moment before her eyes could let go of the scene. Then she watched Crystal pull out onto the street before starting her car. She waved goodbye to Gus, who motioned a high held wave in response.

Pats of Butter

IT WAS ZOEY'S BIRTHDAY. As expected, she found the Javernick Birthday Badge clipped to the outside of her door. It's the facility's tradition that everyone wears one on their birthday. She rolled her eyes and grabbed the badge while wondering if anyone would notice if she just forgot it in her room. But she removed the adhesive backing and stuck it to her shirt. In the early morning hour, she went downstairs for breakfast.

At the bottom of the stairs, she met eye contact with Sam, the site supervisor whom she met the first day. He was sitting at the receptionist's desk watching the building wake-up through an array of cameras. Zoey knew he was a kind person, and he wasn't very large, but she had seen him take command of teenage boys in a fistfight with ease.

"Well, Ms. Zoey. Good morning and happy birthday," Sam said with a wide smile.

"Hi Sam. Thanks." Zoey walked closer. "Are you going to be at the desk all day?"

"No, no. I'm covering the morning shift." Sam closed the newspaper he was reading and rocked back in the chair. "You're up especially early."

"Oh, I'm always up early." Zoey blushed and took another step closer. "When it's nice, I like to go hiking before classes start." She tilted her head toward the doors.

"I could see that, and this place is pretty quiet during this time of day."

"Yah." Zoey was about to leave when she scanned the front of the newspaper. "Hey, what's that article about?"

"This?" Sam held up the paper. "I didn't read that one. It wasn't my thing. Besides, it's just a local newspaper I picked up on the road to Helinas."

"Can I see it?"

"You know I can't give you outside materials. I could get in all kinds of trouble." Sam leaned over and widened his eyes. "And so could you."

Zoey looked around the room and returned her eyes to the newspaper. The paper was the *Lightmeadow Press* and the headline article was "Hometown Healer." Her eyes moved from the title to fixate on the picture of a woman. "I like reading local newspapers," she finally said with a nonchalant raise of her shoulder. "I think it's fun."

Sam leaned back in the chair again and put his hands on the top of his head. "Well, now if I slide it to the edge of the desk." He leaned forward, folded the paper in half and slid it over. "And it happens to disappear. That's a different story."

"Sure, of course," Zoey said, as she set her books on top of the newspaper.

"Happy birthday." Sam turned his attention back to surveying the monitors.

"Thanks, Sam." Zoey picked up the newspaper along with her books and headed straight for the food line. She balanced her books on her tray and was already calculating she could read the article at a stop along the hiking trail. As soon as she got to the table, she slid the newspaper into her folder for safekeeping.

With only a couple of bites left on her plate, she saw Hunter walking in her direction.

"Hey Zoe, happy birthday." Hunter slid his hands in his pockets. "Want to go out to the benches?"

"Um, yah sure." Zoey collected her silverware. "You have good timing; I was just finished."

"Great. I'll meet you by the door."

Zoey and Hunter walked along to their regular bench. They got settled and chatted back and forth, telling stories about their last week in between bouts of laughter. Zoey forgot about the article and the sunshine warmed as the sun moved higher. To her, it felt like only a few minutes had passed when it was time to go to class.

AFTER CLASSES, ZOEY STOPPED by her room. She dropped her books on the top of her desk and the top book on the stack slid to the side. The article was still tucked in the folder where she placed it that the morning. She thought about taking her Birthday Badge off to get some time to herself but the barrage of well wishes from the day replayed in her mind. Everyone already knew it was her birthday. She looked at the folder and sighed.

"Hi. You ready for dinner?" Amber asked.

"Yah, sure," Zoey replied.

Zoey and Amber found places at a large round table with Hunter. The rest of the table filled with other people Zoey had gotten to know. Everyone was joking and laughing when the sound of a chair scraping across the floor grabbed their attention.

"Hey, scoot over. I want to sit next to my friend Zoey," Mar tapped Amber's shoulder with her elbow, her hands still occupied by balancing the chair on two legs.

Amber shot her a disdainful look and scooted to the side. This sent a ripple of people scooting to the side around the table until there was enough room. After retrieving her tray, Mar muscled her way in and pulled the chair closer from behind. Then, to make the scene complete, Site Supervisor Darren was already on his feet, standing about ten paces behind Mar.

"That's what I'm talking about." Mar adjusted in her seat. "Happy birthday," she held up her neon-colored sports drink in Zoey's direction.

"Happy birthday." Hunter also held up his glass.

Everyone else at the table followed suit, and the cheerful toast came to a quick finish.

"Thanks everyone." Zoey grinned and blushed. "I have to say, this is the most birthday wishes I have ever gotten in one day."

Everyone at the table who had been through the Javernick Birthday Badge ritual laughed and empathized with Zoey.

Mar had four dinner rolls lined up on the side of her tray. She picked one up and looked around. Her sight met the butter dish on the other side of the table, so she lifted out of her seat and stretched her arm out, trying in vain to reach the butter dish. The table wiggled and trembled. After sticking the roll that was in her hand partway into her mouth, she had a free hand to stabilize herself while reaching for the dish, but she was still unsuccessful. "Hey, could you hand me that?" she asked through bun and clenched teeth.

Troy, one of their classmates who was sitting across from the table from Mar, looked around before handing her the dish full of square butter pats.

Mar brought the dish closer to her and her other hand slipped off the table, causing her to fall forward. Her muscular legs kept her from baring her entire weight on the table, but when she attempted to go from the partial crouch to sitting back in the chair, she lost her balance again. This time she fell backwards onto the seat and the momentum of her body pushed her into the backrest of the chair. All the while, her hand was holding onto the butter dish that simultaneously flung above her head.

Pats of butter flew into the air, landing on her and half of the table behind her. She looked around, took a bite off the roll that was still in her mouth and said, "Well, I got my butter." Her fingers grabbed a couple of butter pats out of her lap.

By then, Darren was a few steps away, and everyone was trying to conceal their expressions.

"What happened?" Darren stuck his thumbs behind his belt and stared at Mar.

Everyone at the table remained silent.

"You-all can't think throwing food in the dining hall will be overlooked." He scanned around the table, then back at Mar. "I'm afraid I'm gonna have to write a report."

"I didn't throw food. That's crazy," Mar said without returning Darren's stare.

"It looked like you did from where I was standing," Darren replied.

Mar clenched her fists and jaw.

Zoey took a chance and leaned closer to Mar. "What was it you told me the secret around here is?"

Mar slowly turned to look at Zoey. Her brow remained furrowed for a few intense seconds before it smoothed out and light returned to her eyes. "To play their game." She chuckled. "Agree with everything they say and stay away from the meds."

Zoey smiled. "That's right."

Mar nodded. "Damn straight."

Darren did one last survey around the table. "Everything seems calm now." He turned to Mar. "I'll be back for you to review and sign the report."

Hunter dropped his fork on his tray and looked at everyone. "Wait." He paused until he had Darren's attention. "It was an accident. Mar was reaching across the table and lost her balance."

"You expect me to buy that?" Darren kept his thumbs behind his belt and, this time, thrust his waist forward.

"That's all that happened. Really," Hunter said.

Amber surprised everyone by speaking up next. "It's true." She looked at Darren. "It wasn't the politest thing to do, but she reached across to get the butter and struggled to keep from falling on the table. Or someone else."

Darren straightened his stance, and with one last stare, walked away.

"You guys are good friends," Mar announced and scooped a hearty spoonful of mashed potatoes into her mouth.

Hunter held up his glass with a smile. "To good friends."

The rest of the table responded in unison, "To good friends!"

LATER THAT NIGHT, ZOEY tucked herself in a corner of the common area on the resident's floor. It was nice, like a huge old-fashioned den with large tables and plush chairs. Finally, alone, she pulled the newspaper out of the folder and opened the fold. The author of "Hometown Healer" was announced as Lucinda Ambriel. She pulled in a breath and read the article. Often, she had to stop as the information flowed into her brain. The people Joanna saved, her experience when she did a healing, and what people experience when they were healed.

It was like having the answer to a string of terribly odd events and verifying what Zoey knew in the deepest insides of her being. Before she could finish, silent tears of relief tracked down her face and her body went limp. She put her head down on her books and closed her eyes. The detailed memories reclaimed space in her mind, filling in all the nooks and crannies. Everything that happened at the diner with gaining a peace of mind and the lingering tingle in her heart. Followed by everything that happened at the hospital. She cut the memory string off, sat up, and gathered her books.

Zoey went to her room and, as usual, Amber was out and about somewhere else. She exchanged her books for a robe and a towel slung over her shoulder. Finally, she grabbed her shower kit and clean pajamas.

In the community bathroom, the unglamourous shower stalls offered some privacy, and the shower never ran out of hot water. As she stepped into the stall, her memories jumped to the shower at her grandmother's house. That was followed by the memories of the toy piano and her new desire to learn to play. And how she ate different, healthier, with little effort. Then how that change worked into part of the events that ended her up at Javernick. The hot water streamed down on her alongside the rising feeling that the veil had been lifted and there was no turning back. Her shower ritual ended when the lights flashed, telling her it was time to return to her room for the night.

Parent on a Tour

ZOEY WENT WITH THE rhythm of Javernick for a few days, letting everything quiet down after her eventful birthday. Whenever she had the chance, she'd reread parts of the "Hometown Healer" article and further digested its contents.

In her last class before lunch, Zoey remembered how earlier that day she had a strange feeling that something was about to change. She had slowed her steps to focus on the sensation but found it had already fleeted.

Returning to the present, Zoey's eyes moved to the clock on the wall and only five minutes had passed since she looked at it last time. "*Well, nothing's changed yet,*" she thought and shifted to lean her head onto her other hand. She tried to listen to Mr. Dagmire going on about economics, but the words kept turning into a churning drone. In the middle of a particularly long sentence, the fire alarm sounded.

Zoey sat up straight and surveyed the room.

Mr. Dagmire was still holding a piece of chalk in his hand and had his mouth open, as if he was about to say something.

Some of her classmates started getting excited, prattling on about a fire in the building and gathering their things to bolt for the door. Others lounged back in their chairs. The rest looked confused, waiting for direction.

"I'm sure it's just a drill," one lounger said.

Connie's voice flooded the room through the PA system. "This is not a drill. Please remain calm and slowly make your way to the nearest exit."

The students who were excited were already gone. Zoey joined the confused group and merged into the larger flow of students in the hallway. As they were moving along, commotion broke out across the way. Zoey turned to see smoke billowing out of the cracks around the door to the basement level. The smoke was gathering in a small plume. As more people noticed the smoke, the more the chatter rose, and their pace quickened towards an exit.

Connie's voice came over the PA system again, which only amplified the anxiety that was spreading through the evacuees. Zoey scanned around her, and Site Supervisor Sam was directing people out the door. She bumped into another resident and found it was Amber.

"Oh, sorry Amber," Zoey said.

"Wow, it looks like there really is a fire," Amber said.

"Yah, it's really smokey."

They navigated in the stream of students and Zoey slowed a step so Amber could get out the door. They kept going until they were well down one side of the circular drive and merged with everyone else who had already evacuated. All heads turned when two large firetrucks pulled into the side entrance before turning off their sirens. A smaller fire vehicle pulled up the other side of the entrance drive and parked in front of the building. A firefighter jumped out and Sam greeted him. The two talked while pointing around at different areas of the building.

Zoey turned to Amber, but she had disappeared. On her last scan looking for Amber, a woman walking through the crowd held her attention. The woman kept moving closer and stopped next to Zoey. They both stood looking at the building and the smoke billowing out a side window next to the ground.

"Oh, I hope no one was hurt," the woman said.

Zoey examined the woman's silhouette, and she seemed familiar, especially something about the hair.

"I didn't see anything like that going on." Zoey crossed her arms.

"I'm a parent here on a tour. I guess a fire doesn't fare well in getting my business." The woman laughed.

"Do I know you?"

"So glad you asked." The woman conveniently pulled a business card out of her suit pocket and extended it in her direction.

Zoey took the card, and she only had to give it a glance. Her knees flexed, and she bent forward before popping up while squealing, "Lucinda?" She did tiny jumps, still grasping the card. "I recognize you now. And I saw the article."

Lucinda put her hand up. "Yes." Her voice shifted to a lower tone. "But as I mentioned, today I'm a parent on a tour of the building." She returned her sight to the building again.

"Right, sure." Zoey said but she couldn't stop smiling.

"You were difficult to find. But Joanna insisted." Lucinda brushed off the shoulder of her suit jacket. "You just turned eighteen, correct?"

"Yah, this week," Zoey took a deep breath, followed by a slow exhale.

"On my tour today, they told me all about the rules at the facility. They said that all Level One and most Level Two participants who are eighteen and older can check themselves out at any time they want."

Zoey's head got a little light. "I hadn't thought about it. But well, yah. That makes sense." She looked around at her surroundings. "But I wouldn't have graduated high school yet."

"No, but you can graduate from anywhere." Lucinda paused. "You read the article, so you know what led me here, correct?"

"Yah, it has been very…" Zoey looked at the ground. "It's difficult to describe."

"I can only imagine." A group of residents laughing broke the conversation. "The decision is completely up to you. I'm going to return early tomorrow evening and sit in the drive before returning to Lightmeadow. I have an old green four-door Cadillac. From there, Joanna and I would help you with whatever you need."

"Yah, I get it."

"Like I said, it's completely up to you." Lucinda looked up at the trees. "Personally, I'm wondering what are you going to do? Hang out here?" She pursed her lips. "I mean, I'm wondering, is this place really good for you?"

Zoey pulled her arms around her shoulders and nodded that she understood.

"Well, it looks like my tour is finished." Lucinda strolled away, gliding through the clusters of residents.

Zoey looked for a place to sit in the grassy areas surrounding the drive. She spied a spot still in the sunlight and was about to claim her territory when two police cars sped up the drive. They slowed and parked in front of the building behind the small firetruck. An officer got out of each car, and they sauntered into the building.

Zoey sat cross legged on the ground and picked at blades of grass, letting her mind digest the most recent events until garbled noise radiated from a bullhorn. She turned her attention to the noise and waited to see everyone else's reactions. The group gravitated to the sound and seemed to keep flowing away from the current cluster. She got up and followed until she could understand the directions. It was Site Supervisor Darren's voice.

"Okay everyone, let's move on to the athletic field."

Zoey moved forward with the crowd. Just as they were snaking by the entrance, she noticed movements by the doors and halted her steps. One police officer was almost to a squad car while the other officer was exiting the building. The second officer had someone in handcuffs, leading them towards his colleague and the squad cars. They took a couple of steps out of the shadow of the overhang. Zoey squinted and kept watching. It was Mar. Her head was down while being propelled forward by the officer, but no doubt it was Mar.

"Come on now, Zoey." Site Supervisor Sam seemed to appear from nowhere and motioned her forward. "That's not your business."

"Yah, you're right." Zoey took a couple of seconds to accept there was nothing she could do for Mar and continued the walk to the athletics field.

"We need to account for everyone. Let's go, line-up in three lines." Darren further instructed.

Everyone entered the athletics field while one of three teachers checked their names off a master list of residents. Not caring who she sat with, Zoey gravitated to an empty area on the bleachers and waited for whatever was going to happen next.

Hunter gracefully stepped down three rows of seats and plopped down next to Zoey. "Can you believe all this is happening?" He put his arms on his knees.

"No, not really." Zoey thought of her conversation with Lucinda and grinned, but then pulled back while bringing her eyebrows together.

"Is something going on?"

"Did you see? They pulled Mar out of the building in cuffs and put her in a squad car." She scanned the athletics field. "I had ideas but didn't want to think she could really do anything dangerous."

"Mar? No kidding." Hunter leaned back and put one foot up on the bleacher seat in front of him. "It makes sense, but maybe they're just looking at the most obvious person first."

"Yah, maybe," Zoey replied.

The rarely, if ever, seen Executive Director of the facility walked out to a microphone placed in front of the bleachers. Everyone silenced and gave her their attention.

"Hello everyone. For those of you who don't know me, I'm Alisa Brenton, the Executive Director. We have accounted for everyone, and thankfully, everyone is safe." She let a silence pass while she glanced at her notes. "So far we have found out that the fire was contained to the Site Supervisor's break room and the adjoining laundry facility in the basement level."

Zoey and Hunter simultaneously turned to look at each other and their stare held. Neither would say it out loud, but their doubts if it was Mar had fleeted. Site Supervisor Darren must have pushed her past her limit.

The Director continued speaking. "The Fire Marshal is making his inspection and he will tell us if the building is safe for us to return. Until then, we will all wait here and be patient." She swept her eyes back and forth over the crowd. "Thank you."

On the Edge of Evening

THE DINING AREA STILL had the faint smell of smoke that seeped up from the lower level. They had dinner service going early because no one was able to have lunch. Zoey dashed up to her room and sat on the edge of her bed. She looked at her closet and, in a swift motion, grabbed her duffle bag. Once the first shirt was off the hanger, the rest started to come easy. While Zoey was smoothing out wrinkles on a t-shirt, Amber walked in and stopped just inside the threshold.

Zoey kept on neatly folding her clothes and tucking them into the bag.

Amber quietly closed the door. "You're leaving?"

"I'm thinking about it," Zoey replied.

"Well, you're packing." Amber kept her eyes on Zoey while she sat down on her own bed. "Oh, I see. You just turned eighteen."

"That's true."

"You're going to check yourself out. Where are you going? What are you going to do?"

"Wow, Amber, this is the most I've heard you talk." Zoey put another shirt in the bag. "I have plans. This isn't the right place for me."

"I know. I'm pretty quiet, but this is exciting." Amber lifted off the bed and sat back down with a bounce.

Zoey paused her packing to look at Amber. "I'm trying to make a quiet exit, so don't tell anyone." She made the last fold on a pair of pants. "Please."

Amber turned into a vision of stillness. "Oh sure, I won't tell anyone."

"Thanks." Zoey finished packing the last couple shirts laying on her bed.

"Hey, you want to go down for dinner?"

"Yah, sure. I am hungry." Zoey smiled.

AFTER DINNER, ZOEY KEPT packing until lights out. She slept deep that night and was glad to wake up at her usual early morning hour. After eating breakfast, she scanned the room for Hunter. She found him only a couple of tables away reading a history textbook.

Zoey walked over and leaned behind him. "Want to go out to the benches?"

"You know I do." He smiled and started to gather his things.

Hunter held the door for Zoey, and they slowly walked towards their bench.

"You have your books. Is that a ruse or are the rumors that you're leaving today made-up?" asked Hunter.

Zoey groaned. "Amber told you."

"Maybe. Or maybe it was just someone who thought I'd like to know."

"Fine." Zoey sat on the bench and watched Hunter do the same. "I'm leaving." She took a breath. "Yes, I was going to tell you. That's why I asked you out here."

"Uh-huh." Hunter looked up and to the side. "You were just going to take my heart and leave."

"Oh, come on." Zoey playfully pushed his shoulder. A silence passed as Hunter returned to his normal posture. She looked him thoughtfully. "I guess it could violate some imaginary barrier, but we never talked about why we ended up at Javernick."

"Oh, that." Hunter propped a foot on his knee and played with the laces on his shoe.

"Well, it doesn't really matter. We don't have to talk about it."

"No, we can, it's fine." Hunter looked at Zoey. "It's not a long story. I was younger and got into a lot of trouble."

Zoey leaned her arm on the back of the bench. "What kind of trouble?"

"Let's see." Hunter rolled his eyes upward. "I got in a lot of fights and stuff at school. Then I would just do things." He shifted to look directly at Zoey. "My father is a huge CEO, and my mother is a happy little homemaker and party planner. Of course, they groomed me to follow the same kind of life, but that wasn't going to happen. So, I'd get all ticked off and, like, one time, I keyed my father's shiny new Mercedes while it was sitting in our garage." He laughed. "Things like that. It was silly."

"You seem calmer and more in control now. Will you stay here?"

"Why not stay here?" He blushed a little. "It's not a terrible deal. We don't have to cook, but there's always something to eat."

"That's true."

"We don't have to do anything besides keep our room clean." Hunter looked around the grounds. "I mean, it's not much responsibility, really."

"That's true too."

"Besides, I've gotten used to it here. When I leave, I'll have to start over again. Make a new life and find new friends." Hunter leaned back, propping both elbows on the bench. "Why rush that?"

"True, but getting out of here could be exciting."

"I guess." He let his arms down and sat up straight. "When I'm ready."

They watched a bird fly from a tree next to them to another tree across the yard.

"So, what about you?" Hunter asked.

"My turn." Zoey pulled the newspaper out of her folder. "As it turns out, the reason I ended up here is the same reason I'm leaving. It's pretty hard to believe, so I brought this for you." She slid the newspaper onto his stack of books. "I can't really say it all out loud yet, but I have to get used to it." She looked away from Hunter. "I gained this ability to see illnesses in other people's bodies. And I might also be able to heal some of them."

"And you're saying the article is about you?"

"No, but it's about people like me."

"Uh-huh."

She nervously laughed. "When it all happened, my parents thought I couldn't cope with the adult world, so they sent me here."

Hunter picked up his books and flipped open the newspaper. His eyes scanned back and forth half a dozen times before he slapped it closed. He grinned. "I knew you were different from the other girls."

Zoey rolled her eyes, and they shared a laugh.

Hunter continued to say, "No, really. I can see what you're saying, especially given what I know about you."

"Thank you." This time Zoey blushed.

"Thank you for the newspaper. And for trusting me." Hunter leaned in closer. "Since you're leaving, I should thank you proper."

Likewise, Zoey leaned closer to Hunter until their lips touched. It was a short, soft kiss that made her feel warm inside.

Their lips separated, and Hunter grabbed her hand. "I hope all the best for you, Zoe." He stood and pulled her up from the bench. "The cameras are always watching."

They gathered their books and walked back to the dining hall together one last time.

Zoey headed straight to Connie's office to start the check-out process. She took a seat across from Connie who was on the phone.

Connie hung up and, with a hand still on the receiver, looked at Zoey. "Hi Zoey, what can I do for you? Classes start in a few minutes."

"Well, that's just it." Zoey stepped closer to Connie's desk. "I'm leaving today. I want to sign myself out."

"Oh, honey. Not you." Connie motioned her to the seat closer to her desk. Then she mumbled, "Well, then again, you're someone who probably will be just fine."

Zoey sat on the edge of the chair. "Thanks."

Connie was already pulling paperwork out of files. "Do you still have to pack?"

"I'm almost done."

Connie was going across forms, checking boxes, and writing in blanks. "Okay, go finish your packing and clean your part of the room. I'll get your paperwork started." She straightened the stack of papers. "Leave your luggage by the bed and come back here. We'll check you out of your room and bring down your bags."

"Okay." Zoey stood from the chair.

"Are you sure about this?" Connie looked her in the eyes.

"Yes, I'm positive." Zoey grew a broad smile and walked out of the office.

ZOEY'S FINAL PACKING AND cleaning ran into lunchtime and by the time she was officially checked out with her suitcase and duffle bag at her side, it was on the edge of evening. She took the duffle bag and headed for the door. Before pulling the door open, she closed her eyes and hoped Lucinda was already there. The late day sunlight surrounded her, and her eyes had to adjust. Relief washed over her when she spied a green four-door car parked just past the building entrance.

Zoey was almost down the stairs when Lucinda stepped out and used her key to pop open the trunk.

"Hi Lucinda!" Zoey dropped her duffle bag on the sidewalk and returned to get her suitcase. With everything packed in the car, Zoey hopped into the passenger seat, and they pulled out of the drive, leaving the Javernick Center in the rearview mirror.

"Glad to see you could make it," Lucinda said.

"Yah, I'm here." Zoey took in the moment. "Everything seems so strange." She briefly put her face in her hands and rubbed her eyes. "Where are we going, anyway?"

"I told you, we're going to Lightmeadow."

"Yah, sure. But where are we going when we get there?"

"We'll go to Joanna's. I told her I would be by tonight."

"Great." Zoey held up her earphones. "Hey, do you mind if I tune out? I could only listen to my music on off hours."

"Go right ahead." Lucinda smiled but kept her eyes on the road.

AFTER THEY PULLED OFF the exit to Lightmeadow, Zoey was entertained by Lucinda pointing out small highlights around town until they pulled onto a residential street. About five houses down, they pulled into the drive of a large two-story house.

"Here we are, Joanna's." Lucinda turned the car off and leaned forward to inspect the second floor through the windshield. "It looks awfully dark. I wonder if she's home." Lucinda opened the car door in a quick motion. Her long legs brought her feet to the driveway.

From the car, Zoey watched Lucinda briskly walk to the front door, try the doorknob, and do her best to look in the windows. Speeding up her pace, Lucinda went around the back of the house. It wasn't long before she returned to the car, slammed the door shut, and started the engine.

Zoey remained silent as Lucinda backed the large car down the narrow drive at a rapid pace. The tires bounced as the car pulled on to the street.

"She certainly wasn't home." Lucinda put the car in drive. "We'll go to the diner and see if she's there." She flicked the windshield wipers to wipe away the light rain that had started to fall. "I'm sure it's fine, but it's not like her."

They found a parking spot in front of the diner. Despite that the light rain had turned into mature drops filling the sky, Zoey got out of the car. Inside, she followed Lucinda as she walked into the dining area.

"Crystal." Lucinda waved a server over.

When Crystal got within talking distance, she said, "Hi. Are you here for dinner?"

Lucinda waited for her to take a couple of steps closer. "No, I was supposed to meet Joanna at her place, but she wasn't there. I thought you might know where she is."

"No, she left here a little while ago and didn't mention going anywhere." Crystal sunk into her thoughts. She turned over her shoulder and called out, "Hey Gus, did you see Joanna out to her car?"

Gus's voice carried from the pick-up window. "No. She snuck out on me."

Crystal smiled at Zoey. "Hi, I remember you." She tilted her head. "I bet it'll make Joanna happy to see you."

Zoey returned the smile. "Hi, I'm Zoey."

Gus barged into the dining room. "Why are you asking? What's going on?"

Lucinda told Gus about going to meet Joanna.

"God damn it." Gus mumbled as he headed for the side entrance. Everyone heard him fling open the uneven door.

Zoey scanned Lucinda's and Crystal's expressions. Tension had floated to the surface, and they both stared at the location where Gus would return.

The sound of his footsteps entered the room first. He looked at Crystal. "Get back here. All of you."

Zoey's concentration was sharp, she took in everything that was happening like a dry sponge. She followed Lucinda, who was behind Crystal, as they walked through the doors to the kitchen. Gus was already on the phone in his office, and they waited by the door.

Lucinda spoke in a low whisper. "Who would want to harm Joanna? Did anything out of the ordinary happen?"

Crystal frowned a bit. "Well, it was strange. Travis was peeping in the front window the other night." She gestured her chin in Gus's direction. "After the protestors, that really got Gus riled up."

"So, we have the protestors and Travis."

"I guess. Really, it could be anything. Maybe she went to meet Sanders."

"I hope not," Lucinda said flatly.

Crystal swiped a hand in the air in Lucinda's direction, and they giggled.

Gus thumped his way out of the office. He looked larger than life in his white cook's uniform and hands on his sides. "Joanna's car is still in the parking lot," he announced. "To be on the safe side, I called the cops. They're on their way over."

"What?" Crystal said.

Zoey and Lucinda exchanged wide-eyed looks.

"We're going to Travis's." Lucinda turned to leave.

"Yah, let's go check it out." Zoey said while taking a few steps with Lucinda.

"Hold on." Crystal moved closer to them. "Just, ah, be careful. It doesn't seem that Travis has it all together."

"I get it. Thanks." Lucinda started walking and looked back. "I was out at their place once before, on a different story."

What's the Situation?

JOANNA OPENED HER EYES and a shrieking pain in the back of her head radiated all the way to her eyebrows. She tried to check if her head was bleeding, but found her hands tied behind her back. In her mind, she told herself to take a breath and try to stay calm. After finishing the breath, she figured she was riding in the back of a covered pickup truck. The grooves on the floor were made of a jagged patchwork of rust holes and everything smelled like an unkept toolbox.

Her eyes regained their focus in the dark and she used them to search around the covered windows. Then she calmed her breathing and listened with all her might. It must have started raining because she could hear water spraying up from the tires and dampness permeated the air.

The truck slowed and turned a sharp corner. Then it rocked and gravel crunched and popped beneath the tires until the vehicle rolled to a stop. Rain was beating off the top of the cap that covered the bed of the truck. The engine was cut, and she could hear the driver's side door open. As silently as possible, she slid close to the end of the truck bed. Then she turned on her back, her fingers scraping against a rust hole. There was no time to readjust as the footsteps came closer. The steps reached the tail end of the truck, and she slowly pulled her feet back until her knees were close to her chin.

The glass attached to the top of the cap raised, and she saw the driver's torso. Then the tailgate fell open with a thump. As soon as the driver was close enough, Joanna used the strength of her coiled body and thrust her feet into his stomach. He gasped a strained breath, stumbled backwards, and fell on the ground. Panic rising in her throat, she flopped and wriggled to make it to the edge of the tailgate, where she managed to launch herself into a standing position on the ground.

Joanna lost herself in her steaming anger. She could have run away. Instead, she watched the man struggle with having the wind knocked out of him and getting back on his feet. With her arms still tied behind her back, she tapped into self-defense training she learned years ago and swooped her leg under his feet. He fell back onto the rain-soaked driveway with a thump. Before he got his bearings, she stepped closer and kicked him in the ribs. His body convulsed, and he moaned. She had forgotten about the pain in her head, but it reintroduced itself, so she spontaneously kicked him again.

A light streamed through the area, and she looked around to its source. They were at a house and the truck was parked in the drive. A large man walked out a porch door into the backyard. With the light behind him, Joanna could only make out an outline. She tried to focus through the rain falling from dense clouds. The man yelled, "Stop it! What in hell did you do that for?"

Joanna recognized the voice. Soon she could see, it was Travis walking closer. Her eyes darted to the man on the ground, and she put together that it was

Ned. "What do you mean, what did I do that for? That son of a bitch whacked me in the head and threw me in the truck." The memory returning, she looked at Ned and pulled her foot back for another kick.

"No, don't. Stop kicking Ned." Travis put his head in his hands and bent over. "Just stop it," he yelled. "He wasn't supposed to hit you. No one was supposed to get hurt."

Joanna turned to the side. "Then untie my hands." Rain streaked down her face. "Now."

Travis put up his hands. "Yah, okay." He came over and worked his fingers to untie the knots.

Ned stirred on the ground. Travis looked at him. "You better stay down. I'm untying her hands." Travis pulled the rope away from her wrists and wrapped it around his knuckles. Bending over Ned, he stuck his rope-enhanced fist in his face. "When you get up, get in your truck, drive away, and don't come back."

"What is this all about?" Joanna had her hands on her hips.

"It wasn't supposed to be like this. No one was supposed to get hurt."

"Get past that part. What do you want with me?"

"I want you to see my grandmother. Maybe you can help her," Travis said feebly and bowed his head.

"Your grandmother? Is that really it?"

Travis nodded still looking at the ground.

Joanna leaned forward and screamed, "Why didn't you just ask me?"

Travis rolled his head back while shrugging. "I don't know." He looked down again. "I was afraid you'd say no."

"For the love of God!" Joanna looked at the sky and let the rain cascade onto her face.

"Hey, Travis. What are you doing out there and who's with you?" A woman's voice called out from the porch.

Travis looked at the porch. "It's okay honey. We'll only be another minute." He turned back to Joanna. "That's Charlene. She's my live-in." He shifted from side-to-side. "Will you come see my grandmother?"

Joanna managed a half nod.

Travis slowly turned towards the house. Now that Joanna was certain there were other houses nearby, she contemplated taking off down the drive. While she was peering that direction, she noticed two dim headlights appear in the driveway and slowly creep closer.

Charlene had gotten impatient and jogged over. "What's going on out here?" She looked down. "What is Ned doing laying on the ground?"

The headlights crept closer and sent two spotlights on all three of them standing around Ned who was curled up in a ball on the driveway. The car stopped with a slight skid in the gravel. Then the driver's side door flung open. Everyone's eyes got bigger as Lucinda got out, still dressed in a skirt suit with a baseball bat in hand. Walking over, she dug her heels into the wet gravel. She halted a few steps away and used the bat to point at Ned. "What's the situation? Why is this man lying on the ground?"

"That's what I was asking." Charlene took a step closer.

"He's fine. He was about to go home." Travis gave Ned a nudge with his foot.

"Yep." Ned groaned and wobbled as he made his way to his feet.

Travis motioned to the drive that continued around the garage. "You can take the back way out."

On his feet, Ned coughed until he leaned over, and a string of drool hung from his mouth. He wiped his mouth with his sleeve. "It's all good." He feebly waved and staggered his way to the truck.

Everyone watched as the truck pulled around the garage and disappeared.

Joanna stepped closer to Lucinda. "Nice bat. Did you get that from Gus?"

"He found me in the parking lot at the diner and made me take it, said it would help me feel calm. I was happy to have all the help I could get." Lucinda bobbed her head with a chuckle. "What's going on here?"

"It's a long story, but he says he wants me to look at his grandmother." Joanna let her eyes wander to Lucinda's car still idling in the drive.

Lucinda followed her line of sight. "I have the young woman, Zoey, with me. You were right, she has the ability now." She paused. "Are you really going to see his grandmother?"

They looked at Travis and Charlene. Charlene was letting Travis rest his head on her shoulder. He lifted his head, and she went back to lecturing him as they walked back to the house with their arms wrapped around each other's waist.

Joanna and Lucinda returned eye contact and smiled. Lucinda walked back to the car, dropped off the bat, and gained Zoey.

I'm Afraid You're Missing It

JOANNA COULD HARDLY BELIEVE it when Zoey got out of the car. The picture Lucinda had at the interview refreshed her memory, but it felt like more when she instantly recognized the young woman. It was as if they had been close friends for years.

Zoey walked alongside Lucinda and shyly approached Joanna. "Hi. I'm Zoey."

Joanna grew a broad smile, and the skin around the corners of her eyes made creases. "Hi Zoey, I'm Joanna and I can't tell you how happy I am to meet you."

"I'm so relieved to be here. It was like a bad dream." Zoey choked back rising emotion.

"I understand." Joanna allowed a pause to pass. "Come on, are you ready for your first lesson?"

"Um, yah. Okay." Zoey joined Joanna and all three of them walked through the back porch and into Travis's house.

Joanna rapped on the open door to announce themselves. They followed the entryway directly into the kitchen where Travis and Charlene were leaned against the counter. Joanna slowly entered and introduced Zoey and Lucinda.

"Thanks, but we know Lucinda," Charlene said with a snide voice. "And I don't want her staying here if this is going to end-up on the front page of the paper."

"I get it." Lucinda put a hand up. "I'm here as Joanna's friend, nothing more."

"Sure, but I don't think you should go into Grandmother's room," Travis said.

"Actually, it would be a good thing if I stay here and call Gus at the diner. He'll be sending the police out before long," Lucinda replied.

Charlene nudged her chin in the direction of the phone mounted on the wall. "Be my guest."

"Thanks." Lucinda sat partway in the chair next to the phone and pulled a contact book out of her bag.

"Zoey is learning. Is it alright if she comes with?" Joanna asked.

Travis waited for Charlene's nod of approval. "That's fine." He looked up the stairs. "I'll go in first and she how's she's doing."

"Is she at peace with everything?" Joanna asked.

"At peace?" Charlene wondered.

"Yes, does she accept her condition?"

Travis nodded. "I think so. She talks about what she wants to happen after she dies."

"I see." Joanna touched eyes with Charlene, then Travis. "And you still want me to see her?"

"Yes." Travis looked at the floor and swayed his head back and forth. "I need to hear it. The doctors say there's nothing they can do, and I figure if you can't make her better, no one can."

"Okay. I think it's good we can all recognize this is for you as much as it for her," Joanna said.

The four of them slowly departed up the stairs. Travis knocked on his grandmother's door and disappeared into her room. Charlene followed right behind him and left the door ajar.

In the hall, Joanna leaned closer to Zoey and whispered, "If you're comfortable, when I look inside his grandmother, you can too. Just be sure to pull back quickly. I suspect she will have a lot of illness."

"Yah, okay. The first time I saw illness was in my own grandmother."

"Imagine there are roots growing out of your feet, into the ground and to breathe steady. That should help keep from feeling lightheaded."

"Thanks. Yah, I don't like the lightheaded part." Zoey whispered back.

They remained in silence until Travis opened the bedroom door. "She said she would be happy if you visited." He stepped to the side so they could enter.

Joanna found Travis's grandmother in a neatly made bed, sitting up with a bunch of pillows behind her. The bed was dressed in a soft lace comforter that was crisp white. Then the sheets and pillow cases were a sky blue that complemented the dark blue walls. Two soft lamps on dim settings accented each side of the bed.

"Joanna, how wonderful for you to come," Travis's grandma said. She rummaged through a stack of papers and books next to her and pulled out a newspaper. "I read the article about you." She pointed a finger at Joanna. "Good for you."

"Thank you." Joanna blushed. "It's lovely to see you, Lily." She looked at Travis and Charlene sitting in chairs next to the other side of the bed. "Travis requested I come see if there was anything I could do to help with your illness."

"Me? Really? Oh, honey, there's nothing you can do for this old lady," Lily said.

"Well, do you mind if I take a look?"

"Not at all. I get to be one of your special patients."

Joanna turned in Zoey's direction. "This is Zoey." She returned to looking at Lily. "She's learning. Is it okay if she looks also?"

Lily laughed with delight. "This will be the highlight of my week."

Joanna used a hand to guide Zoey to a small chair across from the foot of the bed. Then she gave Zoey a reassuring smile before walking closer to Lily. With her head tilted to the side, she moved slowly, put one hand on the bed, and took a deep breath with her eyes closed. She opened her eyes and looked at Lily's torso until the world around her disappeared. It was as Joanna suspected. The illness was so diffused it filled most of Lily's insides. It was thickest around her abdomen and growing outward almost extending from her shoulders to her hips. It was impossible to distinguish anything that she thought she could heal.

Joanna pulled back and allowed herself to get reorientated. She smiled and looked at Lily. "It is as you say." She took a step closer. "There's nothing I can do. I'm sorry."

"Honey, don't be sorry. Eventually, every soul must fly." Lily used her hands to make an uplifting motion while she grew an animated smile.

"No. There has to be something you can do." Travis put his head into his hands.

Zoey stood from the chair, took a soft step forward and said, "Joanna's right. I saw it too." She clenched her hands before sitting back down.

Silence permeated the room. Lily leaned towards Travis and motioned for his hand. "Now listen." She squeezed his fingers. "I'm old and can't live forever." She looked at Charlene. "Here you have this wonderful woman by your side, and I'm afraid you're missing it." Her eyes moved back to Travis. "Worrying over me. How silly." She flicked her free hand in the air.

"But Grandma, there's always been you. You've always been here for me," Travis said.

"Come now." She sat up higher in her pillows. "You're my boy, and I will always love you. But look at Charlene." With a motion from Lily, Charlene leaned over the bed and extended her hand. Lily took the couple's hands and put them together. "Love her. She's here to be part of you, to be there for you." She leaned back in her pillows and closed her eyes.

Joanna walked softly to stand next to Zoey in the chair. She leaned over and whispered, "This is their emotional healing. As healers, we'll stand here and bear witness until the situation resolves. We'll know when it's time to leave."

Lily continued talking to Travis. "You two are going to have a family and I want to watch you get married before I leave this world."

"Grandma, you know I already have the ring." Travis developed a deep blush and looked away. His head suddenly jerked back in his grandmother's direction. "Wait, you said we're going to have a family. Why did you say that?"

Lily adjusted the top of her comforter. "I'm in this bed most of the time and share walls with your room and the bathroom. I know when everyone sleeps at night, how many naps everyone takes, and when someone is having morning sickness." She pulled the comforter closer to her chin. "I notice these things and you should, too."

Travis looked at Charlene and his face scrunched with emotion. "Is it true? Are we going to have a baby?" He slid his hand up her shoulder.

Charlene rubbed his hand. "I have an appointment with the doctor tomorrow." She gasped and momentarily put her hand over her mouth. "My home test was positive, but I didn't want to say anything until I was certain." She leaned closer to Travis. "It'll be too soon to tell everyone else, anyway."

Travis wrapped his arms around Charlene. They shared peck kisses on the lips and went back to hugging.

Already in tune, Joanna looked at Zoey and they simultaneously met for a brief eye lock. They got up and quietly exited the bedroom. Back in the hall, Joanna slowly closed the door tight.

I Can Help

JOANNA ARRIVED AT THE diner for the Healer's Society Quarterly Meeting. It was strange being at her workplace on a day off, but it got the group away from her house which has served as the hub for all the Healer's Society activities for at least two years now. She walked in and found Zoey at a table expanded by being joined with the nearby tables.

Zoey pulled out an agenda and handed it to Joanna. "Do you want to go over anything before we get started?"

Joanna read over the paper. "No, this is excellent. We wouldn't have made it this far without you." She smiled and handed the paper back to Zoey.

"Thanks, Joanna." Suddenly Zoey's eyes brightened even more. "There's Jessica and her mom." She left to meet them part way.

Joanna watched Zoey greet the mother and daughter with enthusiasm. Not only did Zoey heal Jessica that day in the oncology wing, but it just so happened that she also passed the ability to heal onto the young girl.

Joanna greeted them likewise as they found places around the table. Cassandra, the other healer who was a resident at Javernick Center before Zoey, was the next to join everyone. She was unmistakable, with her shoulder length wavy dark hair and large eyes. "How good to see you again," Joanna leaned in and exchanged a formal hug.

"Cassandra, how are you?" Zoey asked.

"I'm good, still glad to be here, to be part of the group." Cassandra focused across the room. "Here comes Lucinda. The reporter who can track anyone down." Cassandra and Zoey laughed.

Lucinda approached and furrowed her forehead. "What are you two going on about?"

"Oh, nothing," Zoey, still grinning, sat down at the table.

Lucinda plopped her bag down and got comfortable in a chair.

Joanna greeted Lucinda and everyone was shifting their attention to their menus when Brandon appeared. "I'm not late, am I?" Brandon asked, and he looked around the table while he slid into the last empty seat.

Joanna said, "Hi Brandon." Others at the table extended their greetings before Joanna continued, "You're not late at all. We're just about to order some breakfast."

As everyone was eating, Joanna spied Ratlin in the giftshop. He had a box of his latest book and filled the display case. Then he took the remaining books and put them in a stack behind the counter. Crystal approached him, and they greeted each other with a warm hug. Despite Crystal letting her hug go, Ratlin used one arm to keep her close. They talked for a couple of minutes before she took him by the hand and lead him towards a booth in her section. With an enormous smile across his face, Ratlin waved on the way by, and Joanna couldn't help but smile while giving him a subtle wave back.

Once breakfast was finished and the table cleared, Joanna got the meeting started. "Hello everyone and thank you for coming to the Healer's Society Quarterly Meeting. It warms my heart that we are here together." She put her hands on her chest. "Agendas are coming around the table. On first order of business, we have the interviewees selected from the people who contacted the paper because they felt they were also healers." She was scanning the group when, a young boy, ran by holding a metallic red pinwheel. He rounded the corner of the table. Joanna recognized it was Dylan, Travis's and Charlene's son.

"Dylan, stop it," Travis said with a distinct parental tone.

The boy instantly stopped running and looked back at his father.

"Come over here. We're going to sit in a booth."

Still holding the pinwheel in the air, Dylan took off and jumped into the booth next to Charlene.

"Well, it seems everyone is here." Joanna smiled, and the group laughed. "Now, how about that first order of business?"

The group continued working while enjoying each other's company and an occasional laugh. Brandon was about to show everyone the logos he had developed for the society when Dylan made another lap around the table with his pinwheel while making vroom noises.

Travis was on his way to the exit, so Charlene took the helm this time. "Dylan, come over here." She sucked in a breath. "Now."

Dylan ran over to his mother. She leaned over and zipped his jacket. "Now, what did mommy tell you?"

"That we don't run in the restaurant," Dylan replied as he rubbed the corner of his eye.

"That's right." Charlene gave him a squeeze. As she was standing, she noticed the table of familiar faces looking at them. "Hi everyone." She gave them a small wave while Dylan hung on to her leg.

"Hi Charlene. How are you?" Joanna asked.

Charlene took a step closer to the table and Dylan let go of her leg to return his attention to his pinwheel. "I'm good. Real good. Its tuff being a mom but it's more rewarding than I imagined." She looked to the side. "Thank goodness for the rewarding part."

Joanna nodded and laughed along with most everyone else. Over the noise, no one paid much attention to Dylan, who dropped his pinwheel and ran down the row of booths.

Charlene turned to catch sight of her son slipping out the front door behind a couple who was leaving. "No, no. Dylan," she frantically called out. The door closed. Still running after her son, she called to him again. She was almost to the door when she said, "Someone, stop him!"

Not feeling useful, Joanna stood by the table and looked out of the window. Travis was by Charlene's car just across the entrance, but he seemed oblivious to the commotion. Her line of site moved closer to the entrance, waiting to see Charlene, but a car was coming through the drive. Fear jumped into Joanna's heart, and she maneuvered around the table to get closer to the window. The screeching of tires, followed by Charlene's scream, froze her in place.

Crystal was at the booth where Ratlin was sitting, and they had a clear view of what happened. Running closer to the serving window, Crystal yelled for Gus to call an ambulance.

Joanna looked at Lucinda, and they headed for the door. Outside, Joanna did her best to understand what was happening. Charlene was leaning over Dylan, who was lying on the ground, unresponsive. She was talking to him and giving him comforting touches. Blood seeping from a wound on one side of his head had already matted his hair. Travis was standing next to Charlene, his face twisted with countless emotions, but was otherwise motionless.

The man who was the driver of the car kept his distance but leaned over to say, "Oh my, I'm so sorry. He's so little, I didn't see him until it was too late." He sucked in a sob. "I'm so sorry."

Lucinda gave Joanna a pat on the shoulder. "I'll go try to calm down the driver."

"All right." Joanna continued to stand close to Charlene. "Gus and Crystal are calling for an ambulance." She paused. "Try to hang in there. They'll be here soon."

Charlene looked up at Joanna, her eyes tear stained and face pleading. "Can't you help him?" She looked at her son. "Please?"

Joanna leaned over and touched Charlene's shoulder. "I wish I could help, but I can't see injuries. I can't heal them."

A voice projected from the direction of the diner entrance. "I can."

The crowd that had gathered around the scene parted and Ratlin appeared. His face was stone, with his brow clinched and his lips pursed. "I might be able to do something. If it's alright with you." He offered his hand to Charlene.

Charlene hesitated but put her gravel and blood smattered hand into Ratlin's and he pulled her up, then gracefully nudged her closer to Travis.

Travis came out of his state and put his arm around Charlene, who let him further nestle her in the burrow of his large chest.

Ratlin squatted next to Dylan and closed his eyes for a few moments before concentrating on the boy. "Yes, he has a couple of things going on, including a broken leg, but the most immediate is his head injury." He returned to focusing on Dylan's head. "There's a chain of injuries there, but I can help."

"He's so young. Is there a chance you'll pass on the ability to him?" Joanna asked.

"Yes, that's right. If I heal him, Dylan may gain the ability to see and heal injuries." He looked at Travis and Charlene.

Travis pulled Charlene even closer and in between breaths, mumbled something about his son being different, but he eventually nodded. "Yes, help him." He took another jagged breath. "Please."

Ratlin looked to the side before focusing on the Dylan's head. This time, he knelt on both knees with one hand on the ground.

Joanna felt Crystal brush her arm when she came to stand by her side. She grabbed Crystal's hand and hoped with all hope that Ratlin had enough time to do whatever he was going to do before the ambulance arrived. It's not as if the hospital had much to offer a child with a concussion and a residual brain injury. Joanna stared in complete amazement as Ratlin progressed through almost the same behaviors as when they heal illness. All the while, Crystal's hand squeezed hers tighter and tighter.

Ratlin's head jerked backwards, then Dylan's head jerked to the side.

Joanna knelt next to Ratlin and made sure he re-adjusted. "Are you okay?"

"I'm fine." Ratlin re-situated himself. "Maybe I can do something about his leg."

Joanna glanced up and saw Travis still had his arms wrapped around Charlene while they stared at Dylan. Ratlin had just focused on Dylan's leg when the little boy's eyelids twitched, and his head moved ever so slightly. Dylan opened his eyes with a quiet moan, and he looked around, confused.

Travis sighed like a billow and dropped his arms to his sides. Charlene gasped and lowered herself to the ground next to Dylan.

"Mommy?" Dylan looked around some more.

"Yes, honey?" Charlene leaned closer and put a hand on her son's arm.

"Where's my pinwheel?"

Campfire Story

IN THE HOSPITAL WAITING room, everyone sat in two rows of chairs facing each other. Travis and Charlene were in the row closest to the ER doors, where the patients came in and out. Joanna sat next to them while Ratlin, Crystal and Zoey sat opposite. They remained quiet but turned their heads each time the ER doors opened from the inside. The small group's apprehension was different from the rest of the people in the waiting room, because they knew Dylan was okay. Yet, the same as everyone else, they weren't sure what the doctor was going to say about everything.

"Travis and Charlene Hughes?" A voice called out.

"Yes." Charlene said as she took a step towards the doctor.

Travis was also out of his seat but looked back at Ratlin. "Do you want to come with us?"

"No, you go. If they want to do any treatment besides simple stuff, come get me."

Travis turned back towards the door. Everyone watched until the couple disappeared into the treatment area.

"Today has been a complete roller-coaster," Joanna said.

"Hey, what were you going to do? Were you headed to the park or home?" Crystal tugged on the front of Ratlin's shirt.

"I was headed to the park. They wanted me to check on a path for debris and safety, so it would be a solo mission." He crossed his arms. "Seems kind of strange to go now."

"Hey, I have an idea." Zoey said. "Let's all go. We'll go with you."

"You know, I do have a cabin signed out. It's not very big, but I have my camping equipment in the truck." Ratlin leaned back and rubbed his chin.

"Yah, then you won't have to go solo." Zoey scooted to the edge of her chair. "It'll be fun."

"All right, if you-all want," Ratlin said.

"Joanna, are you in?" Zoey asked.

"Sure, I guess." Joanna looked at Crystal.

"Let's do it." Crystal giggled.

"Okay, guess we're all going to take a break and head up to Balmar Cascades," Joanna said with a growing smile.

THE ER DOORS OPENED and a nurse pushing Dylan in a wheelchair followed by Travis, Charlene, and a doctor all came out in a stream. Once they were away from the traffic around the door, the nurse stood in place.

"Well, I'm glad he's alright. He's a very lucky boy." The doctor said as he handed the care instructions to Charlene. Then he shook his head. "It doesn't make sense." He looked at the floor for a moment. "Are you sure no one else was hurt at the scene?"

Travis stepped closer. "No, no one else that we knew about." He half shrugged.

"But there were no lacerations on his head. All we could find was just a small scar. How did he get so much blood in his hair?" An overhead page rang through the speakers and the doctor put up both of his hands. "Never mind. Dylan's fine. Try to get him to rest and follow the instructions about icing the bruises on his leg." He turned and walked back to the ER doors with long meaningful strides.

Everyone gathered around the small family. Dylan soaked in the attention like a rock star, flashing a full smile. Joanna leaned in and gave Charlene a light hug.

Travis looked at Ratlin and put out his hand. "I can't thank you enough."

Ratlin accepted his hand and brought his free hand up to pat Travis's shoulder. "Yes, you're welcome." The long handshake ended. "I'll be in touch," Ratlin said.

Everyone filed out into the sun filled parking lot where fluffy clouds sat on the horizon.

In the Balmer Cascades, the cabin was nested away from city life, off a gravel road and surrounded by trees. Ratlin set up his tent while Joanna, Crystal and Zoey put their things in the cabin. When the day grew late, they gathered around the fire pit.

Ratlin got the fire crackling just a few minutes after twilight. Soon, the light from the flames took over and became everyone's center of focus. Proud of his work, Ratlin stepped back and watched the wood burning until he joined Crystal sitting on a blanket. The blanket, strategically placed, included a large boulder as a back rest. Ratlin leaned into Crystal and slid his arm behind her head. Likewise, she leaned into him and rested her head on his shoulder. Joanna and Zoey were next to them, sitting on the camp stools with a blanket across their laps. Everyone watched the fire mesmerized into silence. The sounds of a million crickets filled the air.

Shifting on her stool, Zoey broke everyone's trance by abruptly saying, "So, Ratlin, what is your story? How did you become a healer?"

"Zoey!" Crystal nervously giggled. "Maybe this isn't the best time or place for that?"

"Everyone wants to know and we're going to find out eventually, so why not ask?" Zoey leaned forward on her stool and the firelight reflected off her face. "So, how about it? Are you going to tell us your story?"

"Only if that's what you-all want," Ratlin said.

"Of course, we're curious. But that's something for when you're ready," Joanna said.

"It's fine. Just let me get some larger logs for the fire." Ratlin stood up. "It's a long story." He came back and let the wood tumble out of his arms onto the ground. He took the smallest log and put it on the fire. Sparks rose up into the darkness. He sat back in his spot next to Crystal but kept his space.

"I'm not sure where to start." Ratlin used a hand to pinch his temples. "Okay, so I was living in the large city of Riverfair."

"Riverfair? You mean the Big River?" Zoey asked.

"The one and the same." Ratlin replied. "I was married. We lived in an expensive high-rise apartment building in the city, and she was an expensive wife." He reached over to grab a long stick from the woodpile and used it to poke at the ground. "It took a lot to maintain our lifestyle and I was working as an accountant for a large corporation."

"I did well and was promoted. My good friend Jackson was the VP Accountant." Ratlin let go of his stick to get up and put another log on the fire. As the flames crept up the sides of the wood, it started to crackle and pop. The smell of campfire was strong in the air.

"Then one day, it all fell apart."

"What do you mean fell apart?" Crystal asked.

"One morning, the CEO and head leadership rushed me into the executive conference room as I was coming into the office. They said that Jackson wasn't there, and they needed someone to review the bottom lines for a stakeholder meeting that afternoon. So, I did." Ratlin sat back down. "What I found was a labyrinth of bank loans disguised as investments and what I assumed to be dummy companies with projected profits. They had inflated the value of the corporation, and given the panic on their faces, they were losing the game."

"They were cooking the books?" Zoey asked.

"Pretty much. I didn't know everything that was going on, but it didn't take much accounting experience to see the numbers weren't right."

"What did you do?" asked Joanna.

"I told them it looked fine for the meeting. Then I went and grabbed this guy I worked with before the promotion." Ratlin looked down, then smiled. "Oh, yah, his name was Allen. He was kind of a wild fellow. Always up for a good time, so we went out for drinks. That's where he told me."

The flames continued licking their way around the wood. A silence rode on the breeze as everyone waited for Ratlin to continue. One log popped extra loud, breaking the pause.

"Allen confirmed all my suspicions when he told me that Jackson had jumped out the twenty-fifth-floor window early that morning."

"How terrible," Crystal said.

"It was hard to believe. So, Troy and I got drunk. Stinking drunk. The night became a blur and I remember walking out of the bar, looking for any sign of a cab. I stepped off the curb and my foot landed halfway on a drain grate." Ratlin chuckled. "At the time, it was enough to send me sprawling onto the street. I heard something in my ankle pop and pain streak up my leg on the way down."

"You got hurt." Joanna said.

"Yep. I was laying there on the damp street with my ankle throbbing in pain. That's when I realized how miserable I was and that I had been miserable for a long time." Ratlin scooted closer to the fire and picked up his stick to rearrange the burning logs. "So, I'm lying there watching the streetlights spin, ready to pass out. I didn't care. Then I heard footsteps walking closer and an old man leans over and stares at me."

"Whoa," Zoey gasped.

"Yah, but then this old man seems to know me. He calls me by name and asks me what the hell I was doing with my life."

"But you didn't recognize him?" Joanna asked.

"No, to this day, I still don't know who he was." Ratlin shook his head. "He held a fancy cane in one hand and pointed at me with the other. He used a firm voice and said that he healed me when I was a kid and if he fixed my ankle, this would be the second time." Ratlin looked around at everyone, who stayed silent. "Then he leaned even closer and grabbed my collar. He told me I can heal people too and if he heals me again, I had better get my act together and start helping people who need it. He let go of my collar with a shove and mumbled something about having to track me down."

"Did you know what he was talking about?" Zoey asked.

"Sort of. I knew as a kid that I saw things other people didn't, like when someone was hurt, but I pushed it down so far that I never gave it much thought until that night." Ratlin rubbed his eyes. "So, the old man healed my injured ankle, and told me that every now and then the ability passes from older men to the younger ones when they are healed. Then he disappeared." Ratlin got up and used his stick to spread out the coals that fell into the bottom of the pit. He stared at the ashes. "That's it. That's the story of how I became a healer." He returned to sitting on the blanket.

"No, wait a minute. What's the end? How did you end up where you are now?" Zoey probed.

"You want the entire ending? You want to hear about the ashes?"

"Yah, of course." Zoey wriggled on her stool.

Ratlin produced his boyish smile. "I wandered around much of that night and finally went home. I told my wife to divorce me and to sell all the investments we had in the company. I told her she could keep all the proceeds. She agreed." Ratlin tossed his stick into the fire. "I guess I wasn't the only one who was miserable. Then I dug my photography equipment out of the back of the hall closet, packed a car full of my things and left the big city of Riverfair."

"Did you ever return?" Crystal asked.

"No, I never had a reason. I started traveling and getting back into my landscape photography. During one of my trips into the Balmar Cascades, I noticed a sign for Search and Rescue Volunteers. I passed the training. From there, I started healing people's injuries when I could." Ratlin sunk into a reflection. "You know, to help get them back to safety." He met eyes with Zoey, then Joanna. Finally, he intertwined eyes with Crystal for a long moment.

Crystal had a grin that grew into a smile. "I knew you had a whole other life."

Ratlin turned to look at the fire until he chuckled. "I guess you could say I traded in my penthouse, fancy suits, and luxury car for a small apartment, camping equipment, and a reliable truck."

"Of the people you healed, is there anyone you passed on the ability to?" Joanna asked.

"I don't think so. Most of the people were older than me or women." Another crackle came from the fire as a log gave way and tumbled into coals. "Until today."

"Oh yes, today." Joanna looked into the flames.

"If Dylan gains the ability, he will need guidance," Ratlin said.

"Don't worry, we have been learning a lot from guiding Jessica. If that's the case, we'll help you with what we know." Joanna looked at Zoey.

"Yah, absolutely," Zoey said.

A Donation You Say?

JOANNA PULLED A COPY of the article Lucinda had published out of the file drawer. She scanned the text until she came to the section about the middle-aged man she healed and what happened to him afterwards. How he had returned to gardening and meditated on his rotator cuff injury. She knew that the man was Douglas Sharp, and he was coming to visit later that day. Everyone worked together to get the house ready and, since then, had dispersed to different places. Zoey was out in the backyard, listening to her music. Cassandra was in the kitchen, keeping an eye on dinner. Ratlin left to see Crystal at the diner. Joanna heard the doorbell and put the article away before going to answer the door.

"Hello. Mr. and Mrs. Sharp. Please come in." Joanna greeted them with enthusiasm. "I'm so glad you're here."

"Please, call me Emily," Mrs. Sharp leaned in with a smile.

"Of course, Emily," Joanna said.

"Yes, and call me Douglas," Mr. Sharp said.

"Hello Douglas." Joanna looked at the couple. "As you know, I'm Joanna. We're glad you're here for a visit, but what would you like to spend your time doing?"

"Lucinda made sure we got a copy of the article and keeps us updated. We've been meaning to come by, thank you for what you did, and see what you have started with the healing center," Douglas said as he looked around the room.

Just then, Zoey came into the entryway, introduced herself, and joined the small gathering.

Joanna led them to the newly renovated first-floor consultation room. "We don't have much to show you, but I'm happy to give you a tour." She reached the doorway and turned to the side. "Here is the consultation room where we meet with potential clients, and it doubles as a workspace."

Joanna guided them through the rest of the tour, including the upstairs where there was an additional workspace, and two bedrooms for healing services and overnight guests. Douglas was endless with his questions, and Joanna was glad Zoey was there to respond about the administrative information. Emily often chatted about the details of the client visit and there was never a moment without conversation. Joanna concluded the tour when they returned to the landing in front of the stairs.

"Would you like some dinner? We planned on having you." Joanna motioned in the kitchen's direction.

Douglas looked at his wife before saying, "Of course, we would love to stay for dinner."

"We're glad." Joanna turned towards the hallway. "We'll be out on the back porch. Cassandra is in the kitchen, and she'll be joining us."

Over dinner, Douglas and Emily got to know Cassandra, and Joanna told the couple about her garden. This spurred Douglas to tell Joanna all about his return to gardening, and Emily joined in to talk about their new recipe adventures. After the talking and eating tapered to a close, Zoey and Cassandra cleared the table and disappeared into the kitchen.

"That was excellent. Thanks Joanna." Douglas stopped. "Since that day in the diner, I've taken on a much better life." He rubbed his wife's hand and looked at her intently.

"It's my pleasure. I'm very glad you are making the most out of everything," Joanna said.

"I would also like to thank you by paying for your services." He pulled a leather-bound checkbook and silver pen out of the pocket on the inside of his suit jacket.

"That's very generous, but we don't charge for our services. If you would like, you can make a donation to the Healer's Society."

"A donation you say?" Douglas looked at his wife and turned back to Joanna while putting his checkbook and pen back into his pocket.

"I'm sorry. Did that offend you?" Joanna asked.

Douglas's eyes were large, but he had a grin on his face. "Not in the least. But a donation is different from paying for services rendered." He rubbed Emily's hand again. "We're headed up to the park for a couple of nights. We'll stop back on our way out of town the day after tomorrow."

"We'd love to have you any time." Joanna glided her eyes from Emily to Douglas, looking for a hint of what they were thinking.

"I have a proposition for you." Douglas leaned over the table and tapped his finger in rhythm with his words. "I want you to think big." He sat back and looked above the trees. "The sky's the limit." Then his eyes returned to Joanna's. "And when I come back, give me a business proposal of what you want to do with this charity. I'll look at it before I make my donation."

"I don't know what to say. This is a bit irregular," Joanna said.

"There's nothing irregular about it at all." Douglas let go of a belly laugh. "A person should know what a charity is going to do with their money." He turned to his wife in a smooth motion. "Well, dear, we've taken up enough of Joanna's time today." He stood and put his hand out for her. "And she has a lot of work to get started on."

"She sure does, dear." Emily smiled and, with the help of her husband's hand, glided out of the chair.

Joanna walked the couple to the front door. She did her best to be graceful, but her mind was a scatter of details about Douglas's request. After farewells with the couple, she ran into the kitchen where Cassandra and Zoey were still hanging out.

"You will not believe what happened."

"What? What?" asked Zoey.

"Douglas wants us to put together a business plan because he would like to make a sizable donation." Joanna put her hands to her warm cheeks.

Zoey and Cassandra cheered and grabbed each other's wrists. They cheered more and jumped in a circle. "This is unbelievable!" Cassandra said. They stopped to look at Joanna, who was standing with her body and face rigid, and the room fell silent.

Joanna looked back at the two women. "We need everyone who is free to be here as soon as possible."

IT WAS JUST BEFORE dawn and Joanna had already brewed coffee. Rather than return home, Cassandra stayed in one of the client bedrooms. Barely awake, she staggered into the kitchen.

"Help yourself to coffee and fill your plate. There's left over fruit and cheeses from yesterday." Joanna was comfortable in her favorite chair at the kitchen table and took a sip from her coffee mug.

Cassandra gathered her breakfast and sat across from Joanna. "I think we came up with a good plan for today. Now we just wait for everyone to arrive." Cassandra took a sip of her coffee and closed her eyes. She opened them and continued, "You and Zoey work together really well. It'll be great."

"Thanks Cassandra." Joanna picked at her cantaloupe. "It just dawned on me; I've gotten to know you a little bit over the years, but we haven't talked about how you became a healer."

Cassandra continued concentrating on her breakfast. "It's not a fun story."

"I can only imagine."

"Well." Cassandra picked up her coffee mug. "When I grew up, my father was mean and controlling, and my mother wasn't strong enough to handle it. Together they had plenty of money but made terrible parents."

"I'm sorry." Joanna put her hands together, giving Cassandra her full attention.

"Then one day, about when I was twelve, I didn't feel good. Soon I was throwing up and my side hurt. It hurt terrible; sharp on the inside." Cassandra sipped from her mug. "My parents ignored my complaints and said I would be better in a day or two.

Thank goodness my aunt came to visit me. She was married to my father's brother." She set her mug on the table. "My aunt took one step into the room, and said, 'Oh my goodness.'" Then she told my uncle to get out, and not to let anyone in. Once we were alone, she healed me. The relief from the pain was incredible."

"Did you see your aunt again?"

"I saw her a few times, and she tried to help me with being a healer, but suddenly they stopped coming to visit. My father said they moved away, but I knew better than to take his words at face value."

"I see."

"I kept looking for my aunt and my father found out. He was furious. Then, as I got older, it became clear seeing illness inside of people wasn't going to go away. So, I figured, since my aunt was a healer, then there had to be other people like her in the world. I put ads in the local grocery store rags and sometimes the local newspaper looking for others. The newspaper was a mistake because my parents found out, and that's when they sent me to the Javernick Center."

"How long were you there?"

"Oh, not that long. Maybe a year. But it was long enough to teach me not to talk about seeing other people's illnesses. Once I graduated high school, my mother came and signed me out." Cassandra peered into her coffee mug as if the coffee inside was telling the story. "Then she supported me so I could move in with a longtime friend of mine, and she never said a word about it to my father. That really surprised me."

Cassandra leaned back in her chair. "After that, I went on with life. I figured it was a strange ability, and

I just had to accept it. I never had healed anyone and after so much time had passed, couldn't put it together that it was possible." She leaned forward into the table. "That is, not until Lucinda was standing on my doorstep."

Joanna blinked her emotions back. "I'm so glad we were able to find you and that you are part of a society with other healers just like you." She kept her eyes on Cassandra even after they heard the knock on the front door.

"Hello? We're here." Crystal's voice carried from the entryway.

"Come on in. We're in the kitchen." Joanna replied.

Crystal made her way to the kitchen, where she exchanged greetings with Joanna and Cassandra.

Ratlin appeared behind her and joined them in the conversation. "Congratulations Joanna. It seems you walked into something very fortunate."

"We'll see how it turns out. It's very exciting." Joanna had a beaming smile. "Help yourself to coffee and a plate. We have a work area set up on the back porch and Zoey will be here soon." Joanna stood from her chair. "I'm going to finish getting ready."

We Need Space

BY THE TIME JOANNA made it to the porch, Cassandra, Crystal, Ratlin and Zoey had settled around the long table. In preparation, Zoey had arranged a whiteboard at one end. Near the whiteboard were neat stacks of papers and a basket of writing utensils.

Joanna stood next to the head of the table. "As you know, an old client of mine, Douglas Sharp, is interested in making a donation and wants us to make a business proposal that outlines what we would do with the money."

"How big of a donation?" Crystal asked. "I mean, what are you talking about here?"

"He didn't give a specific amount. He just said to think big and the sky's the limit. So, I think if we move forward, we should put together the biggest plan we can be successful with and complete a business case for in one day."

"You know him best; does he seem sincere?" Ratlin asked.

"Oh, he's sincere. But I'm also sure as a businessperson, he wouldn't have a problem turning down something he didn't think would work."

"Fair enough. Most of us are here." Ratlin looked around at the group. "You've already put effort into getting started. I don't see why we wouldn't move forward."

"Yes, let's get started," Cassandra nodded at Joanna.

"Yah, of course," Zoey said. "Brandon will be here soon, and Nancy and Jessica will be here later today."

"Great. Zoey, Cassandra, and I worked out an approach." Joanna passed around a handout for everyone. "Zoey is going to take the lead at the whiteboard." She sat back into her chair.

"Hi everyone." Zoey waved. "So, on the paper is the Healer's Society Mission statement, which includes two primary goals. One, to bring healers together to work in support of one another and improve on our abilities. The other goal is to heal people and support them in achieving a high-quality life." Zoey drew a line down the middle of the white board. Then she wrote healers on one side and clients on the on the other. "We're just going to brainstorm for a few minutes and write what we offer to healers and clients on a list."

With the lists complete, Zoey stepped back and looked at them with the group. "It seems we're lacking on the client side."

"Yes, we don't have any training for them," Cassandra said.

The group fell silent until Brandon came walking around the back of the house. "Hi, everybody."

"Brandon, you have incredible timing." Joanna went to greet him at the top of the steps. "Come find a seat. We were just working on something that could use your input."

"Awesome." Brandon took the closest seat. "Nothing like diving right in."

Joanna nodded. "Yes, I guess you're right." She looked at the whiteboard. "Take your time and as a client who has been healed, let us know what you think."

Brandon took a few minutes and, when he finished, looked at Joanna. "Well…" He leaned forward. "Similar to what you-all have described, clients go through an adjustment afterwards. I was drawn to things like the artwork. It felt strong and it was confusing. I also experienced peace and satisfaction in a new way. There is no training or guidance for that, like you have planned for new healers."

"That's true." Zoey stared at the list. "Even as a healer, the changes in my eating and wanting to get more involved with music were an adjustment."

"It sounds like we could have training not just for that, but we could combine them with things like art, music, and, maybe, meditation," Cassandra said.

Joanna leaned closer to the table. "The meditation part makes me think of Douglas. Lucinda told me how he visualized an injury healing, and he felt it helped him get better more quickly."

Ratlin chuckled and rubbed his chin. "One woman I had healed told me she got a terrible sinus infection, and she imagined a bunch of Pac-Men eating the bacteria."

"Did it make her feel better?" asked Joanna.

"She thought it did." Ratlin nodded. "She said that she did the meditation a couple times a day, and her infection got better in a week or so, without taking antibiotics."

"That's like my meditation teacher." Cassandra looked around the table. "She used to teach courses on Meditation for Healing. I could get in touch with her."

"Yes, absolutely," Joanna met eyes with Cassandra.

"Zoey could take more music training and add music therapy classes," Crystal said.

"That would be totally cool," Zoey replied.

"Yes, put it in the budget," Joanna looked at Zoey, then turned to Brandon. "Would you be interested in teaching some basic art and help with the adjustment training?"

"Sure, that would be awesome," Brandon replied.

"And Joanna, you could teach gardening and use your garden for hands on training," Cassandra said.

"Oh, yah. That's perfect." Zoey slid into a chair. "We could have sessions for clients that include meditation for healing, music, arts, gardening and adjusting."

"We would be the Healer's Society Healing and Learning Center," Joanna said with a far-off look. "When we have the space, we could include the client's family members who are interested."

"When you-all have space?" Crystal asked and everyone at the table looked at each other.

"We need space!" They all said in unison and laughed, aside from Joanna who had become an intent observer.

"Where are we going to find a suitable building this quickly?" asked Joanna.

"We could just put money in the budget and find one later," Zoey offered.

"Yes, we could do that, but it would be great if we could come up with something," Joanna said, but her thoughts were still working on embracing the idea.

"There are the offices next to Lightmeadow Press. They've been empty for a while," offered Brandon.

"What about something, I don't know, warmer? More natural," Joanna said.

"I know, what about the Dewayne Estate? It's on the market," Crystal asked.

"You mean the Dewayne Bed and Breakfast?" Joanna leaned over with her eyebrows raised.

"I know which one you mean, the huge estate and guest house," Zoey said.

"It's a pretty big house and two buildings are a lot to maintain." Joanna crossed her arms.

"This isn't like you. It's not like you're going to lose your house. That place would be perfect, plenty of room, green space, and next to the meadow." Crystal grinned and twirled a curl around her finger.

"The green space would be great for a lot of things including a garden. And we could even rent tents and have outdoor events," Cassandra added.

All eyes turned to Joanna. She knew they were right. "Let's check it out," she said.

For a moment, the table erupted with a small cheers and joyful laughter but then Zoey zipped out of the room. "I'll go call the realtor," she said.

"I'll see if I can find Travis. Maybe he can inspect the place and give an estimate on construction costs." Ratlin followed Zoey's trail.

"I'll get ahold of my meditation instructor and start compiling the information we have started." Cassandra gathered the whiteboard.

"I'll start cleaning this up and get lunch ready so everyone can keep working." Crystal cleared plates and cups.

Joanna found herself alone on the porch. She looked around the yard while remembering playing in its nooks and crannies. The more she looked, the more her throat started to tighten.

Zoey's voice carried from the inside of the house. "Come on, Joanna. The realtor's picking us up in a few minutes."

Home of its Own

JOANNA HAD EVERYONE GATHERED in the living room where they waited for the Sharps. Zoey had neatly stacked copies of the proposal on the kitchen table, and Cassandra had prepared breakfast. The coffee pot had been going strong since yesterday and most everyone already had a mug that morning. Just after a burst of laughter, a car pulling into the driveway halted their conversation. The stillness lingered as they heard car doors closing and voices drawing closer to the front door. Then the doorbell chimed throughout the house. Joanna looked at the group, straightened her dress, and opened the door.

"Hello, Douglas, Emily, so nice to see you again," Joanna extended an arm, welcoming them into the house.

"We're glad to be back and I see we have an entire group to greet us," Douglas scanned the living room.

Joanna reacquainted everyone and introduced Ratlin and Crystal, who didn't meet them during the first visit. Douglas pulled Joanna away from the rest. "Is your proposal ready? Is there a place where I can read it, to take it seriously?"

"Sure. We have the back porch set-up for breakfast. You can read it there while everyone visits."

"Perfect. Tell my wife to let me know when everyone is ready to eat."

Joanna grabbed a proposal and made sure Douglas was comfortable before leaving him alone.

The sounds of vibrant conversation traveled down the hallway. Joanna wrapped her heart around the gratitude in her chest as she neared the room. She merged into a conversation with Emily and Cassandra. Crystal came around and made sure everyone had something to drink. Ratlin and Zoey were huddled together on the couch, amusing themselves with a Rubik's Cube. Emily excused herself to check on her husband. Joanna took advantage of the moment to tell everyone Douglas was reading their proposal.

Emily returned with a classic smile and asked if they were ready for breakfast. The group gathered and made their way to the porch. Crystal and Ratlin brought out the food. The fresh ingredients had everyone guessing what herbs were in the eggs.

Douglas wiped his hands on his napkin and set it to the side. "I've read your proposal and I'm impressed." His expression stayed steady. "But I also have a few questions."

"I'm glad the proposal impressed you. Please, feel free, ask us anything," Joanna took a bite of pastry.

"Okay, first. Cassandra." He looked up from the proposal. "Becoming a Meditation for Healing instructor? Are you sure you are up for it?"

Cassandra's eyes popped open. She looked around and set down her fork with grace. "Yes, I know it's not a popular thing right now, but I've been practicing meditation for over ten years. One of my mentors is excellent. She's the one who agreed to start the program here and train me."

"Uh-huh. And what are the trainer's credentials?"

"I'm not sure who she studied under." Redness traveled up the side of Cassandra's cheeks. "But I know her because she was part of a research study on healing meditation where I was a participant. At that time, I didn't know I was a healer, but it makes sense I was drawn to something along those lines." She shifted to face Douglas more directly. "And from my perspective, because I learned the meditation techniques before learning how to use my abilities to heal someone, gives me unique insight into how the one method blends into the other."

Douglas pulled a smile up from one side of his mouth. "Great." He dropped his smile and flipped through a few pages of the proposal. "And Zoey." He looked at her. "The cost of the college courses is an investment. Why should your boss invest that much in you?" He rocked his head in Joanna's direction.

Zoey finished her drink of juice. "Because I'm committed, and I'd be good at it. I have the perspective of a healer and have studied music history. I'm also a skillful pianist. The music therapy is a perfect fit." She glanced around the table. "Besides, I couldn't imagine letting myself, the other healers, or our clients down."

Douglas brought his smile back and raised his eyebrows. "Great, that's just great." He closed the proposal. "One last question. Crystal."

Crystal was enjoying a bite of strawberry waffle. She swallowed and looked at Douglas. "Yes?"

"I don't see you in the proposal. Who are you?" Douglas looked around and everyone chuckled.

"That's easy." She smiled and looked at Joanna. "Joanna is my longest and best friend." She wrapped her hands around Ratlin's arm. "Ratlin is my boyfriend." She looked back at Douglas. "And Brandon, who you read about in the proposal, is my brother."

Douglas adjusted in his chair. "Well, I see why you're here."

With another chuckle in reaction to Douglas's comment, the group conversation rekindled for a brief time. Then with things quieting, Crystal began clearing the table.

Once she left, Douglas looked at everyone. "If you don't mind, I'd like to talk to Joanna alone for a moment."

As everyone stood and gathered their plates, Douglas looked at Emily. "You're welcome to stay." Then he reached for her hand.

"Thanks, sweetheart." She accepted his hand but stood up from her chair. "I'll let you two talk things over. Besides, Ratlin and Zoey were playing with a puzzle game that looked like fun." She went into the house with a giggle.

"Joanna. Your proposal is good." Douglas pulled his pen out of the pocket inside his suit jacket. "But it's missing a few key things." He flipped the pen around and handed it to her.

Joanna took the pen and pulled her copy of the proposal open to a back of a page. "Yes, please tell me." She looked at him with open eyes.

"The biggest thing is to get a couple of graduate students to conduct research on what you're doing. It's publishable stuff. Someone will jump at the chance." He shifted and put a foot on the opposite knee. "But work it out first that they will give you data summaries, help with grants, and stats for brochures, stuff like that."

"Okay." Joanna was already writing down the information.

"The research with the healers is important, no doubt. This has nothing to do with your abilities, but my hunch is the meditation, the self-healing, also has potential for large impact."

"It took me a while to put it all together, but yes, it has the potential to change the way people think about health and healing." Joanna tapped the pen on her paper. "It has the power to tap into the body's power to heal and make people an active part of their own healing."

Douglas pointed at her. "Now you're getting into it." He extended a hand to retrieve his pen. "Well, my wife is probably ready to head home."

"We've been glad to have you back," Joanna said, lowering the pen into his hand.

With the pen and part of Joanna's hand in his grasp, he leaned in and said, "Add those things to the proposal. Take a few days then send me the new version."

"Yes, thank you for telling us what it needs."

"You do that, and I will fund the entire amount for your first year. And based upon what is in your proposal, the agreement will be renewable for up to five years."

Joanna tried her best to conceal her escalating emotion, but cupped a hand over her mouth before saying, "Everyone will be overjoyed."

"You have a sound fund-raising plan. You won't need me that long." Douglas rose from his chair and took slow steps into the house.

The steps faded and Joanna couldn't hold back anymore. She got up from the chair and looked around the yard the same way she did yesterday. This time she could feel the emotions rise through her chest before entering her throat. Her home started with her grandmother, who was a healer. It continued to spread its warm embrace around Joanna, and it stayed to become the protector as the group took shape. It housed life and love. Now the Healer's Society was going to have a home of its own.

Full Stride

JOANNA COULDN'T REMEMBER BEING so nervous. She had never done anything like this and hoped she wouldn't burst into tears of joy in front of everyone. It took close to a year, but the old DeWayne Estate was now the new Healer's Society Healing and Learning Center. She walked closer to the meadow where the sun was creating a glow around everything that thrived in its realm and soaked in the inspiration.

"It's time," Zoey said.

Joanna took a deep breath and looked at Zoey. "Here we are." She took a step. "It's so hard to believe."

The two of them walked side by side and the stage grew closer and closer. Zoey had led planning the opening ceremony and did an incredible job. A small stage surrounded by seats was setup on the lawn next to the end of the driveway. The outer rim of the area was decorated with bunches of brightly colored balloons that bumped and swayed in the wind. Finally, there was a double layer of party streamers tied to two entryway lights that flanked each side of the drive.

They rounded the corner, and Joanna could see the crowd. She scanned the faces. Some were so familiar they had become family, while others were faces that she just recognized, and a few were faces she didn't even know. Zoey led her to the few steps onto the stage.

"Are you good?" Zoey asked.

"Uh-huh. Thanks," Joanna choked. She continued to the small podium and placed her speech on top. She looked at the crowd until everyone was silent and still in their seats.

Joanna spoke into the microphone. "Hello and welcome." She smiled. "The Healer's Society is so delighted you could be with us to celebrate the new Healing and Learning Center." She raised her hand in the building's direction.

The crowd let out a short applause.

"In this moment of reflection, I think back to when the healers weren't together and the challenges we faced." Her eyes glided across Zoey's, Cassandra's and Ratlin's faces. "Because of the strength and dedication of the first few of us who found each other, the Healer's Society came to be." She let her eyes continue across the entire front row of healers, some of them alongside their parents. "Please help me give a well-deserved thank you to all of them." She gestured for them to standup and joined in clapping with the audience.

Before the applause from the crowd became silent, she said over the sound, "And since then, we also have welcomed five more healers. Please stand up." Joanna held her hand toward the new healers that they found through responses to the "Hometown Healer" article. The new healers stood and acknowledged the crowd.

Joanna let the applause end. "Now that the society is formed and growing, never again will healers be left alone to struggle against their precious talents."

Joanna looked into the crowd at Lucinda and the paper's investigator, Zach. Then she spied Gus sitting tall with a proud look displayed on his face and couldn't help but grin. "At the beginning, I thought that bringing healers together was the principal goal, the sole mission of the Healer's Society. It is a large item; without healers, the society wouldn't exist." She chuckled. "Even so, there was the other side of the equation. The client. We have no one to heal without the client."

Joanna scanned Brandon's face who was sitting with Crystal. "The person who has healed from illness or an injury has so much to learn about actualizing themselves and what their body already knows about healing." She looked down at her speech for a moment. "Our learning center will include training for clients and their family. They will learn side-by-side with healers and the healers will learn from them."

The sound of the balloons bumping in the wind took over a brief silence. "Never again will a client be left to face the changes brought on by a healing alone. And even more so, clients will learn to be active participants in their future healing. So, never again will treatment be something that is done to them. They will have the knowledge of how to activate the body's own healing process."

Joanna looked over the crowd. "Perhaps one day our clients will teach others how to take part in their own healing before they experience the symptoms of illness or to rapidly find relief from an injury." She leaned her head to the side. "Who knows? The future is wide open to think about health, healing, and well-being in a new way."

Joanna caught Douglas in her peripheral vision who had a large grin that grew in sync with the heightening applause from the audience. She spoke into the microphone with robust, "We look forward to dedicating our new meditation room to Mr. and Mrs. Douglas Sharp later today. Without their support, none of this would have happened." She motioned her hand towards the couple, who smiled and nodded at the crowd.

Once the last claps started to fade out, Joanna said, "Now let's have the next generation of healers who will fill the center with healing and learning cut the ribbon."

Travis and Charlene led Dylan, who did become a healer, out in the front of the crowd. After they passed by, Nancy walked along with Jessica. Zoey was waiting close to the streamer with oversized plastic scissors. She handed one to Dylan then one to Jessica and encouraged them forward. Jessica, being older than Dylan, took her time and let him get into place first.

The two looked at each and nodded. In unison, they clamped the scissors shut. The streamer gave way and separated into pieces that carried in the wind a short distance before resting on the ground. Dylan and Jessica turned back to face the applauding crowd. Dylan raised his hands above his head while Jessica stood with her hands clasped in front of her. Both had smiles so large they took over their faces.

"The Healing and Learning Center is open! Let's enjoy more events and lunch in our lovely green space by the meadow," Joanna announced.

Filled with energy from the applause radiating from the audience, Dylan took off running towards the building. In reaction, Jessica and her mother looked at each other with amused smiles. Then Jessica shrugged before sprinting up the driveway, where in no time at all, she hit her full stride.

About the Author

Laura is the author of *Exploratory Tales* and *The Five Dimensions of Self Awareness*. Academically, she has a master's degree in Philosophy and served as Adjunct Faculty in the Humanities. When she isn't reading and writing, she spends time connecting with others, enjoying nature, and watching all kinds of documentaries. To subscribe to *Laura's Latest* newsletter or contact her visit: www.lauraclementzauthor.com

One Final Note

Thank you for reading, *The Healer's Society*. Reviews mean a lot to authors and other readers. If you enjoyed the book, please take a moment to leave a short review at Amazon.com and if you are member of the community, at Goodreads.com.